BRING YOUR BEACH OWL

OWL STAR WITCH MYSTERIES BOOK 7

LEANNE LEEDS

Owl Melt with You
Paperback - 978-1-950505-66-1
Published by Badchen Publishing
14125 W State Highway 29
Suite B-203 119
Liberty Hill, TX 78642 USA

Copyright © 2022 by Leanne Leeds

For permissions contact: info@badchenpublishing.com

CONTENTS

BRING YOUR BEACH OWL

CHAPTER ONE

"*I*'m going to have a hard enough time cleaning out this Jeep after this vacation," I told Althea as another crispy golden fry pelted Ayla in the head. "Do not throw fries at each other in here. I'm serious."

My sisters Ami, Althea, and Ayla—twenty-two, seventeen, and fifteen respectively—were so excited they were practically vibrating as we drove southeast toward Cocoa Beach. It was the middle of March, which meant that the Space Coast was once again inundated with visitors. This year that included the four of us.

"I still can't believe you got Mom to agree to this," Ayla said once again, still chafing at the memory of our mother's lecture about how dangerous Florida beaches were during spring break. "She hates the beach."

"She doesn't hate the beach. She thinks the beaches are for rituals, not drinking until you vomit," Althea piped in from the back seat. "I think she's a little worried that people might get crazy around the full moon, and—"

"We only got to go because she wanted us out of the house," Ami finished for her. "You realize that, right? Astra just hit her at the right time with the right question. I think Mom, Aunt Gwennie, and Aunt Gertie are having a week-long sister conclave of their own."

"Have you ever been to a conclave?" I inquired, not paying much attention to their discussion.

Even after a week without rain, the air outside was salty and Florida humid. The Jeep's air filter had been replaced, but the SUV still reeked of something reminiscent of the inside of an old locker or a locker room, the odor of sweaty gym clothes. I turned up the air conditioner for a few seconds to get rid of it.

"You're not even listening, are you?" Ami laughed when I didn't respond. "We're a permanent cabal. Cabals are much better. They're more exclusive." She paused for a few moments as a gas station whizzed by. "I wonder what Amelia's like now. I haven't seen her in ages."

The one aspect of the trip that Mom insisted on was that we stayed with Amelia Arden, a distant cousin of ours who lived in Cocoa Beach. Amelia hadn't been a big part of any of our lives —at least not in the last twenty years or so. But she was a witch, and she was family. Mom reasoned that it would be safer for us. "It's preferable to staying in a hotel with spring breakers swinging from the rafters," she said, shaking her finger at us. "If you want to go, that's the deal."

Our mother and Amelia's mother were cousins, and according to Mom, they were joined at the hip as kids—at least until Amelia's mother died.

"I think I see Archie." Ayla craned her neck out the window. "He's flying so low. How does he not get shot by some overly eager hunter?"

"All Florida raptors are protected under the federal Migratory Bird Treaty Act and under Florida law. This means the birds themselves, their nests, and their eggs are protected," Althea, the book-smart sister, explained. "No hunting. No trapping. No collecting. No harassment.

Though you can get a falconer's permit and hunt with them if you want."

"I wonder if Amelia will be there when we get there?" Ami commented from the back. "It was weird, her teleporting you a key. I'd hoped we could all hang out a little bit, and now she's making it sound like we may not even see her."

"Yeah, to be fair, it did seem like she didn't really want to see us," Thea agreed.

I glanced in the back through the rearview mirror. "She's probably just busy. Mom didn't exactly give her much of a choice."

My eyes drifted back to the road, and I frowned.

My sisters weren't wrong.

When I called Amelia the week before, she was curious as to why we were coming. Why now, why this year? I told her the truth: Mom, who is always concerned about crowds, had convinced herself that a full moon in Aquarius meant that people would be less likely to be violent or dangerous on Cocoa Beach's beaches. Amelia didn't seem pleased with the response.

In fact, she seemed a little suspicious.

Amelia spent the majority of our call pelting me with questions like, "What did Mom expect?

What exactly were we doing there? What did we need from her?"

I stammered through most of the conversation, trying to reassure her we didn't really want anything—certainly nothing for her to be concerned about. I told her that Mom was just being Mom and wanted us to stay with family, that we had no plans, no expectations, and that we would just hang out and have fun.

Aunt Gwennie retrieved an envelope that flew out of the communication cauldron minutes after we hung up. The address of a beachfront condo and a note about where to park was written hastily on the outside. Inside the envelope? Two keys.

"She's going to be there, I'm sure," I told my sisters, trying to sound more confident than I felt. I took a deep breath and tried again, keeping my eyes on the road. "And, look, if she's not there when we arrive, we'll still have a condo to hang out in while we're visiting." I raised my eyebrow. "Someplace warded. Which, I suspect, is what Mom was after all along, anyway."

* * *

THINGS WERE GOING RELATIVELY WELL in my life. I'd turned my paranormal military experience and psychometry ability into a psychic consulting position with the Forkbridge Police Department. Emma Sullivan, my best friend, was an excellent detective (and, luckily, the person I worked with most of the time). I even had a boyfriend, Jason Bishop, a handsome middle school teacher and the only son of Cassandra's Mayor Lillian Thornton, the famous psychic.

Not bad for a thirty-something witch bounced out of the military thanks to a paranormal coup just one year ago.

A witch with no prospects and no pension, I reminded myself.

While my life appeared to be going well, my family had been having difficulties recently. And it wasn't just my sisters and me this time.

My mother, the high priestess of the goddess Athena, and her ever-faithful sidekick, Aunt Gwennie, recently encountered the ghost of their third sister, Aunt Gertrude. (Well, Mom came face to face with the ghost because she could communicate with them. Aunt Gwennie must have used Mom as a go-between.)

This reunion was not particularly welcome.

Mom had kept Aunt Gertrude out of the family's sight. By magic.

Like, banished her own sister.

Anyway, Aunt Gertrude and my mother had a falling out decades ago over someone that died. Aunt Gertie believed that the past was the past. The past belonged in the past, and the dead belonged in their graves, and Mom was a terrible person for barring her own sister from having relationships with her nieces over something as trivial as a corpse.

Mom, of course, disagreed—but Mom didn't count on Ayla and Aunt Gertie teaming up to break the banishment.

Mom, Aunt Gwennie, and Aunt Gertie were now at odds with each other. All day and night, there was constant bickering, complaining, and disagreement. It was a bad situation, but that's what happens when you're a witch—even a high priestess—and your family is involved in a decades-long quarrel. You can't avoid it no matter how hard you try, and if you do, it comes with three times the drama.

Well, you can't avoid it *unless* you take a vacation to Cocoa Beach for a week of sun and fun.

Which I decided to do.

Before I clocked all my elders with a silence spell.

"This is going to be fun," Ami said. "I can't wait to hang out with Amelia."

"I've always liked Amelia." Thea sighed. "I'll be so bummed if she isn't there."

"So, where are we now?" Ayla asked. "I haven't been south of Orlando in, like, a million years."

"We're not all that far south of Orlando," I told her, spotting the exit to get on Beachline Expressway. "We're east, really."

"I saw a sign for Cape Canaveral!" Ayla squealed so loud I jumped in surprise. My youngest sister had become a sullen, serious, snarky teenager in the last year, and it had been an eternity since I heard the kid squeal. "Are we going to be close to it? Can we go? I've always wanted to go there!"

"We will be close to it, and yeah, we can probably go," I told her, nodding.

"Sweet!" Ayla looked happier than I'd seen her in ages.

"I still can't believe Mom let Ayla come with us," Ami said with a sigh. "I keep thinking we're going to run into a magical sign or something directing us to bring her back to Forkbridge."

"We wouldn't have to go back," Thea said.

"Amelia has a communications cauldron." A communications cauldron allowed witches to communicate with one another through the mist. Kind of like a Zoom call. The one thing it had that the humans didn't? The ability to teleport items—and people, if it was big enough—across space in an instant. "That's probably why Mom wants us staying with cousin Amelia. So she can snatch us home in an instant. If I was Ayla, I'd be worried."

"Oh, come on! How is Mom supposed to punish me for my bad attitude when it was Aunt Gertie using me to talk to her? Something Aunt Gertie wouldn't have had to do if Mom hadn't used that banishment spell." Ayla rolled her eyes. "Besides, what's the point of being a death speaker if you can't talk to ghosts sometimes? It's not my fault I'm better at it than Mom."

"I wouldn't mention that to her the next time you two talk," Althea smirked.

"I can't believe Aunt Gertie used you to get the banishment lifted," Ami told Ayla. "That really was kind of brilliant on her part, if you think about it."

"You guys, you realize we've been on vacation for over an hour now, and all we've done is talk about Mom, Aunt Gwennie, Aunt Gertie, and their problems?" I asked my sisters. "We're on vacation, without them. Even Aunt Gertie decided to stay back at the house so they could deal with their issues. Let them deal with their issues, let us be grateful we don't have any right now, and let's start enjoying the vacation, shall we?"

My three younger sisters nodded simultaneously. The discussion swung easily between what we would do when we got to Amelia's condo and whether or not the wind would be our friend or our enemy tomorrow when we rented a boat.

The sun was poised over the horizon, its brilliant light glimmering off the buildings in the distance as we drove the last few miles to Cocoa Beach.

* * *

HALF AN HOUR LATER, I pulled into the parking lot of the beachside building. I easily found the guest parking space assigned to Amelia's condo and eased the Jeep into the spot.

Every level of the five-story, square beachfront condo building had a large balcony with a view of the water. The entire structure was a bright yellow color that stood out against the sky and sand, and it appeared well kept with neat landscaping. Frogs gathered under the bright parking lot lights.

"Oh, wow. Is that a private dock?" Althea asked, craning her neck toward the beach.

I followed her gaze to a long dock that extended out over the water.

"Look at the size of that boat!" Ami said, pointing toward a forty-foot yacht.

"That's not that big," Ayla said with a shrug, but her eyes sparkled.

I took the keys out of the ignition and got out of the car. My back was sore, so I stretched and walked around to the other side. "Look, there's a lifeguard tower, too," I said, pointing to a white platform set up on the beach side of the condo, just to the side of the dock.

"I do believe it is," Ayla said, squinting out of the open car window. "And I think it's a private beach."

Ami looked impressed. "She's right on the ocean?"

"Yep, she is." I nodded. "She told me she's got a killer view." I opened the car door and reached in to help Ami out. Ayla and Thea were already standing next to the car, examining everything.

"Excuse me!"

Althea looked around. "Did you hear something?"

"Excuse me! No, no, no. Excuse me!"

I turned to find a sour-faced woman hurrying toward us, determination echoing with every step. She beelined with the intensity of a predator chasing its prey, but her expression said she'd caught it.

"Hi! Can I help you, Ms....?"

I waited for her to introduce herself.

She arrived out of breath and stood close enough I could smell a powerful scent of sweat and ocean. "You girls, you can't park here!"

I glanced at the envelope and then down to the number on the parking space. This was exactly where Amelia had told us to park. In fact, she was pretty insistent about it.

I looked back up at the woman.

A tight bun held her gray hair back, and her blue eyes were slits in her long face. Her narrow nose, thin lips, and small eyebrows made her look like a shark. She was wearing a button-up top two sizes too small and a pair of tan shorts much too tight.

I smiled. "Hello. I'm sorry, ma'am, your name is?"

I kept waiting for her to give me her name, but again, I didn't get it.

"That is a private parking space," the woman said coldly, nodding toward a sign set at eye level near the entrance to the condo building several feet away. "Are you sure you're in the right place? There are no rentals here, no Airbnbs, all owner-occupied. We don't have spring break on this part of Cocoa Beach, you know." Her eyes were a cold blue, her purplish lips a tight line. "I don't know if you young women can *read*, but it says parking for condo residents only."

"I understand, ma'am," I told her respectfully. I pulled out the envelope Amelia sent and held it up for the woman. "Our cousin lives here, and she directed us to park in this spot—"

"Your cousin? Lives here?" she asked, her voice firm and clear, and kind of angry like she was annoyed that her words were being ignored. "Who is your cousin?"

"Amelia Arden."

She folded her arms across her chest. "Impossible. She would have told me." An owl screech startled the woman out of her judgmental stance for a moment, and she glanced up fearfully. "I thought those things sleep during the day."

"Some owls do. In any case, I promise you it's not impossible. Amelia's our cousin, and we're staying with her this week," I said in an even tone, hoping to appeal to the woman's sense of logic. "This is where she directed us to—"

She cut me off with a repeated, "You can't park here," as if she thought starting the whole conversation over would get her what she wanted. "You are going to have to move your car. There's no parking for renters there." She glanced at my uniform for a long time, longer than some random human could be expected to.

I was so annoyed, I didn't notice.

"You're not listening to me, ma'am. We're not renting this place. She's not renting this place. She owns the condo. We're her guests."

"I'm sorry, but I *don't* believe you." She pursed her lips again. I fought the urge to reach out and smooth her top lip to remove the permanent frown on her face. "I know all of the owners in this building, and they would have told me if Amelia had cousins…like you."

I blinked.

That statement didn't even make sense.

We just got here.

How would the other owners know anything about us?

I felt like I'd stepped into the twilight zone.

"Ma'am, she sent us here, and she said to park in this spot." I held up the envelope again. Between asking me questions, Amelia had warned me that the condo association was very nosy, that I might be questioned and I should avoid saying much of anything to anyone I didn't know. "She said to come right to this spot. We're not trying to cause any trouble, but—to be frank —I also don't want my Jeep towed."

"It's *your highness*, first of all. And no, I'm sorry," the woman shook her head. Her expression migrated from angry to worried. "You'll have to move your car." She pointed to a rectangular space three spots away. The spots between the one I was in and the one the woman pointed to were empty, and I could see no rhyme or reason for the woman's directive beyond the fact that she enjoyed ordering people around. "You can park over there."

I looked at the luggage we'd already pulled from the Jeep. "But—"

"No buts. Just move your car. Now." Her lips were tight, her eyes narrow.

"Excuse me, ma'am? You said you know all of the owners?" Ami asked, her blue eyes wide and friendly. "I'm just curious. How many are there?"

"Just six, including Amelia," the woman responded after a pause.

"Althea, Ayla," I said. I turned to Ami. "Let's get the luggage up to the condo."

Ami nodded, and she and Althea pulled out the luggage we took from the back of my Jeep.

"Six owners, huh?" Ayla asked, her voice light and conversational. "Wow, that's not a lot of owners for a building that big. The condos must be huge."

"It's a nice building," Althea added. "And I'm sure the view is stunning."

The sharp-faced woman looked at the buildings around her, her eyes still narrowed. "It is a nice building. All owner-occupied. Nicer than these other ones," she said. "And it has a stunning view." The tone of her voice was...odd. Defensive, almost, even though there was nothing personal or accusatory in Ayla or Althea's comments.

"It's lovely," Althea told her. "We feel very privileged to be staying here."

For a brief second, it looked like her eyes might have softened ever so slightly. "That must be nice. I felt that way once," she said. But then her lips tightened again, and she nodded slowly. "But you still can't park there."

CHAPTER TWO

The woman—whoever she was—disappeared with a hurried gait back into the building once the car was in the spot she'd picked for us. Ayla remained fixated on the spot where the woman had gone, chewing a lip and worrying.

"What? You look like you want to say something." With Ayla's heightened ability to see and hear ghosts at the drop of a hat, any look of concern on her face might be an issue I needed to know about. "Something wrong?"

"The entire situation was bizarre. Why was she so concerned with where we parked? And if Amelia was aware enough to warn you about the condo residents' nosiness, why didn't she simply inform Queen Nosy over there that we were arriving?" Ayla turned and looked at me with a raised eyebrow. "The whole thing doesn't add up. And did you see how tense she was? She was tense."

"Don't go kicking over rocks, Ayla Arden!" Ami said, hitching a duffel bag on her shoulder. "Sun. Fun. Fine dining. Lying on a beach so my poor, pale body can get a little bit of color. Maybe we'll see some sea turtles on Cocoa Beach...um, beach. The Kennedy Space Center. That's why we're here. This is supposed to be a break from cases and customers and Mom and—"

"And you're right about all that." Althea shrugged. "But the kid's got a point. That was weird."

"Shake it off, both of you. Ami's right. Let's try and have a good time for a change." I pulled out my phone and hit Amelia's number. "Let me just call Amelia and let her know we're here. I don't want to just burst into her apartment unannounced."

"She probably has a doorbell," Althea said.

I listened while holding my finger up to Althea. I got Amelia's voicemail and left a brief message informing our cousin we'd arrived, taking care to describe where we'd parked and the vehicle, and informed her we were on our way upstairs.

The lobby of the beachside condo was better appointed than the outside would suggest. It was large, with gleaming marble tile and a tall marble reception desk with aquariums recessed into the walls along each side. The reception desk stood on a white base, and an elegant crystal chandelier hung above.

"Oh, snap," Ayla said, staring. "There's a doorman."

A young man with dark hair sat behind the desk; he looked up and smiled as we entered. The lobby had a pleasant, clean scent of fresh flowers and polish. In fact, it seemed to be bathed in fragrance, a dozen different scents in a dozen different combinations.

"You must be Amelia's cousins from Forkbridge," he said, standing up. "I'm Charles. Welcome to the Elysium Condominiums." Doorman Charles, a tall, muscular guy in his mid-twenties, ran a hand through his slightly damp hair before extending it to shake mine. The fish sparkled like diamonds in the aquarium behind him.

"Thank you." I shook his hand, grateful that he didn't use a lot of product in those curly locks of his. "Nice to meet you. I think we're a little early."

Charles smiled. "Nothing wrong with that." He glanced at his watch. "Amelia said you'd be here about now. I have your keycards."

"Keycards?" I had a key. Why would we need keycards? "For what?"

"The elevator, to start. They'll get you access to everything the building has to offer." Charles smiled, his teeth shining bright white. "You'll love it. Amelia has a full kitchen if you need it and prefer to cook, but we also have a continental breakfast here just off the lobby." He handed me four plastic cards. I looked at them—they were each assigned to one of us. I passed them out. "All important information is on your keycard—your room number, any numbers for food delivery, etcetera."

"This seems more like a resort than a building with condos." Althea's voice had a distinctly suspicious ring to it.

"We pride ourselves on being a five-star property, ma'am," Charles said. "Our third-party rating agencies have given us five stars in every category, including resident services. If you need help with anything, anything at all, just call me, or use the phone next to the elevator in your condominium."

"An elevator?" Althea asked with surprise. "In the condo?"

"Yes, ma'am." Charles touched Althea's arm. "Anything at all, ma'am. I'll make sure you get to wherever you want to be in this building."

"She's seventeen," I deadpanned, glaring at the doorman.

"Yes, but I'm not twelve, and I didn't need you jumping in there," Althea snapped at me with an annoyed glare.

My response didn't rattle him. "Of course, Ms. Arden. Amelia let us know exactly who you all were and everything we might need to know to make your stay as comfortable as possible." Doorman Charles bowed slightly. "And, of course, if you need anything, I'll get it for you. That's why I'm here."

I got it.

He only said it five times.

"Thanks, Charles." I pulled my keycard back out of my belt and headed toward the elevator. The picture on the front suggested the key unlocked the elevator, pool, gym, sauna...for a small building with six owners, this place sure was heavy on the amenities.

We piled in the elevator.

"There are no buttons," Ami said with surprise.

"I think you use that key card thing over there." Althea pointed toward a glass square with a flashing red light.

I swiped the card in front of the glass, the light turned green, and the elevator whirred to life. It announced audibly that we would be traveling to the top floor, and the computer-generated voice welcomed us again to Elysium.

"Amelia didn't mention she was in the penthouse." Ayla looked around with a curious expression.

The elevator shuddered and lurched to a stop. The lights dimmed.

The doors opened.

* * *

"AMELIA'S RICH?" Ayla gasped. "I mean, she has to be, right? Rich people live like this. And, like, only rich people."

The condo was everything I imagined a modern luxury beachfront penthouse to be. The main room was an open expanse of chrome, glass, and white leather furniture that wrapped around a large, modern kitchen equipped with multiple fridges, ovens, and stovetops. On the right, there were large windows with views of the beach. On the left, there was a set of sliding glass doors.

The door to Amelia's bedroom, which we discovered moments after entering the penthouse, was at the end of a short corridor lined with marble floors, mirrors, and intricate tapestries. Her bedroom was beautiful, but it was still small compared to the overwhelming living room. She had nothing more than a bed, a dresser, a desk, and a small closet. The bedroom, like the rest of her living space, had views of the beach.

The entire penthouse was a wonderland of opulence.

"I don't know the details, but, honestly, I never asked her. I mean, who asks something like that?" I looked out the windows that wrapped around the condo. The view was spectacular—the ocean was right there.

"It's a small apartment building," Althea said with a gulp. "I would never have guessed something like this was here. It looked—"

"Normal?" Ayla asked. "Middle class?"

Althea nodded silently.

I remembered, vaguely, seeing Amelia at family gatherings when we were both children. Her mother's mother was my grandmother's sister, and so we were second cousins. Aware of each other, yes. Still family.

But not particularly close.

I knew little about her adult life. Her mother died when she was young, and her father had remarried. I think he lived in Chicago, but I couldn't remember for sure. I definitely couldn't recall any stories of the family striking it rich.

But then again, we were a witch family.

Money mattered little to us.

Magic did.

"This is just—" Althea took a deep breath. "I'm honestly a little embarrassed that I'm so shocked, to tell you the truth."

"I'm kinda jealous." Ami fanned herself with a hand. "It's so nice in here!"

"We don't exactly live in a shack, you guys," Ayla told Ami and Althea.

Ami pointed at the dedicated wine refrigerator. "We don't live like this."

I couldn't disagree.

"Okay. We've oohed and ahhed. So, now—" Ayla took a breath. "What do we do?"

"Well, I need to wave to Archie." I gestured

toward the glassed-in patio that ran the length of the living room. It was surrounded by a waist-high glass wall, through which I could see the large trees. "He doesn't know which condo is Amelia's." I walked toward the door that led outside, a set of double doors with a sturdy lock. I looked through the glass and waved my hand.

He spotted the movement in seconds, and I watched him fly toward me, looping in wide circles above the condo. He dropped toward the condo, crashing into a glass patio table.

"It's about time," he snapped, his beak clicking. "If I ate one more frog, I would have had to wait until morning. I wouldn't have been able to get any lift." He jumped down to the patio and stepped toward me, fluttering his wings. "At least there are a lot of them."

"Sorry about that." I gave him a half bow. "I was a little bit delayed." Sometimes it was easier just to apologize, even if I had nothing to apologize for. The bowing to his highness, the divine owl, probably didn't hurt, either.

That appeared to appease him. "I suppose you have your reasons." The owl's head swiveled from side to side. "You have entered a place that is clearly a manifestation of one of the new gods. That's probably distracting."

Ami looked confused. "What new gods?"

"What new gods?" He fluffed his feathers, preening for a moment. "Why, money, of course. Money is definitely one of the new gods. This place is practically perfect. I'm not sure if you're aware, but perfect costs a lot." He hooted. "But, of course you're aware of that. I just told you." Archie stretched a wing out and gestured around. "You people are lucky you have me."

Ayla snorted. "I wouldn't call it luck, exactly."

Archie glared at Ayla. "Just because you have an elder of your own now, you're going to start questioning Athena's wisdom?" He flung his wing toward me. "I practically just got this one to admit she's a witch! Don't you start!"

Ayla stared at Archie for a moment and then closed her mouth.

The owl looked around with a satisfied expression before turning back. "So, what have you learned?"

I blinked. "Learned? What do you mean, learned?"

"About why we're here."

"We're here for vacation," I reminded him. "I learned how to get into the condo and, lucky for you, learned how to open the patio doors.

Beyond that, I'd like to learn where we should go for dinner."

Archie looked at me for a moment, then blinked. "Vacation?" He hooted with laughter. "That doesn't sound like a waste of time at all. Absolutely not."

Ayla looked at me. "Why did we bring him again?"

"For his comedic timing," I replied with a shrug.

Ami and Althea both snickered.

"And," Archie continued, "because I'm pretty sure that you're actually supposed to be here. Otherwise, you wouldn't be here. That means I'm supposed to be here. You know, since you're supposed to be here."

"We're supposed to be here for vacation, birdbrain," Althea said, her hands on her hips as she glared daggers at the owl. "You know, four sisters bonding. During spring break. Which none of us have ever gotten to go to because Mom is a paranoid witch taskmaster with an inordinate need to control her daughters' lives."

"That feel good?" Ami asked. "Getting that off your chest?"

"Well, he's only here for Astra's star power," Althea told Ami, her arms crossed. "Nothing's glowed; you haven't flipped over any cards. Detective Sullivan has managed to go several hours without calling Astra and asking her to read an object. Ayla hasn't seen any ghosts that need our help. So, you know, as far as I'm concerned, he's yanking our chain, and this is vacation. No work. No cases. Nothing to figure out other than directions to the best beachside dining." She glanced out the window. "And the sun's almost set. So let's go."

The owl cocked his head to the side. "You know, I've heard that before—that I am only here because of the star power—and I'm not sure I agree with it."

Althea snorted. "Of course, *you* wouldn't."

Archie glared at her for a moment, his eyes narrowing. "It's because you don't like to be wrong, isn't it? The attitude. It's all that book learning. You know too much, and now you think you know everything. You just can't stand to be wrong."

"Vacation, Archie." Althea walked to the elevator and waited.

"Look, I'm not just here because of your star power." Archie hopped onto the back of a chair and lifted one wing, gesturing for a second. His big eyes stared deeply into mine. "I am here because, as it turns out, there's another reason why you're here. Not just spring break."

"Okay, why am I here?"

He folded his wings back and tilted his head. "If I knew what it was, I'd tell you. But I don't know." Archie fluffed his feathers. "But I know there's something. I can feel it."

"If you don't know what it is, Archie, we may as well go out to dinner. I'm not going to go tearing through the island looking for some case to get into." I scratched the owl behind his ear, and his eyes half closed. I lowered my voice. "And you're here because we're family, right?"

Archie stared into my eyes for a few more seconds, then gave a single hoot, ruffling the feathers on his head. "Fine. Fine. You win. You ready to go eat?"

Althea waved her card in front of the elevator panel and stepped in as soon as it arrived. "Finally. By the way, Archie, I've eaten frog. I don't recommend it."

Archie clicked his beak. "Clearly, you haven't eaten the right kind of frog." He took off toward the open glass door.

* * *

CHARLES RECOMMENDED a tiki seafood restaurant near the pier. Without pausing for our response, he called the restaurant and made reservations for the best table just off the beach—even ensuring there would be a perch for Archie at the table so he could join us.

You know, the owl we'd snuck in.

And hadn't mentioned.

My sisters didn't seem to notice the odd acknowledgment of my familiar's existence, and I kept my surprise hidden beneath a bland expression.

But...what the heck?

Maybe the Elysium Condominiums was not just a beachside home for wealthy people that didn't want their ostentatiousness displayed on the outside of the building. The small number of actual units in the large building, the amenities, the doorman's awareness of my raptor companion all seemed...odd. Even everyone's aversion to giving their name, or full name, seemed slightly off from a regular human building.

Though, you know, humans could be weird.

I'd heard stories about secret magical communities that existed in the human world. Some claimed they were descendants of historic covens, while others claimed they were simply families who preferred to live apart from the rest of the paranormal world. I knew a few people who said their parents had told them about such groups, but I'd met no one who had actually visited one.

When I asked my mother about their existence, she shut down my questions with a curt, "No one knows where they are, and it's best not to look."

I frowned.

Well, I mean, technically, Arden House was one.

But this? This was six separate people or families all living in a building.

With a doorman.

It seemed different.

I wasn't sure how to feel about this island just yet, so I accepted the directions with thanks and said nothing. I resolved to say nothing at dinner, too—I wanted my sisters to get at least one fun evening if, as Archie claimed, something was coming.

One thing I have to admit—Charles had great taste.

The food was delicious, and I thoroughly enjoyed it. I took advantage of the opportunity to sip the fruity drinks, listen to the steel drum and ukulele music, and pretend for a brief moment that I might actually be at the start of a real vacation.

I smiled at the other diners and looked out at the incoming tide.

I breathed in the evening ocean air and tried to relax.

I smiled at Archie and talked with my sisters about trivial matters.

But as the sun set completely over the ocean, I scanned the shadows on the beach, wondering what was out there in the dark.

CHAPTER THREE

$\mathcal{I}$ plopped down at the breakfast table with my sisters Ami, Ayla, and Althea. Archie was probably off eating every last frog he could find, no doubt. The table was crowded with plates of eggs, fruit, bacon, biscuits, toast, and pancakes. I helped myself to a plate of eggs and bacon and a slice of toast.

Ayla's mouth was already full when she nodded at me and swallowed. She leaned forward, elbows on the table, and tentatively wiped her lips with her fingers.

"So, I have a question for you." She moved her napkin and lowered her voice, reflecting the seriousness of the question. "Why did you join the military?"

Ami and Althea turned their gazes toward Ayla and me. Thea studied me with mild interest, while Ami gave me an apprehensive look.

I shrugged and took a bite of eggs. They were delicious, perfectly prepared, with fragrant toast and smoked bacon. "I wanted to serve and protect the paranormal world. Ministry life made sense for me. Someone has to defend the supernatural world from people that want to exploit it." I looked around. "Who cooked? This is great."

"I did," Ami smiled. "Thanks."

"You're trying to change the subject," Ayla told me. "I know darn well whatever you claim you wanted to be when you went in? The fact is you wound up working for the people that corrupted the supernatural world for hundreds of years."

I sighed.

Great.

It was going to be one of those mornings.

It shouldn't have surprised me. My sisters still lived with my mother their entire lives. Mom was vehemently opposed to my Ministry military life, the Witches' Council, and my position within both. Each time we spoke over the years, she would rant about how the Council only cared about their betters and how the military was a breeding ground for intolerant witches. She would make snide comments about my choice to continue on with my career instead of coming home.

That Mom's viewpoint wouldn't have some effect on my sisters wasn't terribly realistic.

"That's a very simplistic view of things. The Witches' Council wasn't all bad, and the people we chased weren't all good. I caught a lot of people that did some really terrible things to paranormals and humans alike," I pointed out. "We served an important purpose and stopped some serious crimes."

Ami asks, "Like what?"

I took a big swig of orange juice. "Once, I went after a vampire that was turning human teenagers without their consent. Another time, there was an elf stealing human family's wealth and leaving the entire family with their minds wiped clean." I waved my fork at Ayla. "Think about the power we have and the damage we could do if we didn't care who we hurt. Who's going to stop us, the humans?"

We all laughed at that idea.

"I don't know that Mom hated your job as much as she claimed. I think she was just always so upset that you never came home for holidays," Althea said as she played with her eggs. "Though I did once hear her tell Aunt Gwennie you stayed in Imperatorial City because you were embarrassed to come home and defend what you were doing with your life."

"That is not why I rarely came home. I had a job to do, and people in the military don't get holiday vacations very often. That's just not how it works," I tried to explain. "The Witches' Council couldn't afford to waste any time or resources. Anything we missed on our day off could mean some paranormals getting hurt or killed. Catching the right people on the right days was hard enough."

"At least Mom could never stay mad at you for long," Ami said. She looked like she was on the edge of saying more but stopped. "So, I had a thought. What do you think that key is for?"

"I'm not sure I know what you're talking about," I answered, genuinely confused.

"The key Amelia sent through the cauldron." Ami gestured toward the front door. "Charles gave us electronic cards to get into the apartment, right? There's not even a front door. The elevator just opens into the place. If that's the case, though," she said, leaning in toward me and lowering her voice, "what is that key for?" Ami sat back and smiled at me like she'd just scored big points in a debate. "Honestly, you're the one that works with a detective. I'm surprised you didn't pick up on it."

"I'm on vacation," I told her. "I didn't think about it because I don't care."

"Maybe it's just a spare?" Althea suggested.

Ami shook her head. "Spare for what? There's no front door. There's no lock."

"I don't know. She didn't send more information than the envelope, the parking directions, and the key," I admitted. "Maybe it's for something else?"

"Well, obviously. Like what?" Ami pressed me.

"I don't know, a jewelry box?" I offered. "A cupboard? A hidden entrance to a hidden room?" I shrugged. "Maybe there's a locked liquor cabinet in here somewhere, and she wanted to make sure we had access to the booze. It is spring break, after all."

Ami shook her head. Her eyes rolled as her voice came out in a cynical tone, laced with disbelief. "It doesn't make any sense. And Astra, you did say Amelia acted weird on the phone. Maybe you should pull a glove off and give it a peek."

"I don't know her well, so maybe that's just how she is. But yes, she hung up on me before I could get much information, and she said zip about a key before she flung it into the cauldron." I took another sip of my orange juice. "But honestly, I don't think it's all that mysterious. It's probably just a spare key to something in the building. Maybe it gives access to the garden courtyard in the back of the pool."

Ami stood up, plates in hand. "Whatever it is, I'm going to go out there and take a look. I'd like to take a walk around the grounds, anyway, before we go to the Space Center today."

Althea rose from her chair and headed for the door. "I think I'll come with you."

"Sounds good. Let me go change, and I'll meet you at the elevator."

Ami left the kitchen. Althea followed. I heard drawers open and close as they looked for clothes to wear. Thankful that we avoided this turning into the case of the mysterious key, I stood up.

"You don't like talking about the military, do you?" Ayla asked, still sitting in her chair and eating pancakes. "You get this weird look on your face whenever I ask you about it like you sucked on a lemon."

I sat back down. "That's not true. I don't mind talking about it."

Ayla snorted. "You're a terrible liar."

I smiled, with a hint of sadness in it. "Okay. Yes, it was just a little uncomfortable talking about it, to be honest. I was chatting with Emma the other day, and I realized that I'm no longer the same person that I was while I was in the military. Sure, some of me is still there and will never change, but the person that I used to be is gone. I'm not bitter, though. I'm just...a bit disappointed in the way my service ended."

"What do you mean?"

"All of us deserved better. My soldiers deserved better. Heck, I deserved better. We signed up to risk our lives for people, somehow got blamed for things we had no control over, and *then* got kicked to the curb without the benefits we were promised. It's a little galling if you want to know the truth."

"Typical government," Ayla said. "Though it shouldn't be typical. It wasn't right. You were promised benefits and great jobs and help with housing, and then you were put out in the street. Just like that." She snapped her fingers. "Not cool."

I shrugged my shoulders. "You're right, but you being right doesn't change the fact that I still feel that disappointment. Still mourning the loss a bit. I still want to know why the people I pledged to protect and serve were never really behind me. If they had been, it wouldn't have happened. Well, at least not the way it did. And those are answers I'll probably never get."

Ayla put her fork down. "I'm sorry, Astra. You deserve so much better than a crappy government that doesn't care about you."

"Thanks," I said, and I meant it.

"You have to accept the loss, though. That's just part of life. You have to move past that and focus on what comes next."

"I am. And what comes next is vacation." I gave her a brief smile and then changed the subject with as much force as I could muster. "You probably need to get cleaned up and changed. The later we go, the more crowded the Space Center is going to be."

She stood up and started walking away. "Okay. It shouldn't take me long."

My anger throbbed like a tiny red devil hitching a ride on top of my head. It whispered to me of all I lost during my military service and that my life was only half as good as it could be. Despite everything I'd gained since coming home, I still wasn't at peace.

What had been taken from me and the

promises broken still left a bad taste in my mouth.

* * *

"D<small>ID</small> you know this is NASA's primary launch center?" Ayla asked us as we wandered through the Kennedy Space Center visitor complex.

"I did not," Ami murmured, watching a video of a space shuttle mission.

It was like being in a different world. There were exhibits of all the space missions and pictures of all the astronauts who had been to space.

Ayla was especially amazed by everything. She kept stopping to look at things and asking random employees what they were. The NASA employees would enthusiastically explain in detail, and then she would want to go over and look at them closer. It was slow going.

I felt a sudden pang of guilt watching Ayla's obvious excitement.

It was insane to me that she'd lived an hour and a half away from this place, and yet Mom never thought to bring her. My years of public school brought me to this place several times, and it was a great experience. As a child, I stood beneath the United States' very own Saturn V rocket—it'd ferried man to the moon several times. The shuttle Discovery was next to it, and several other space shuttles and rockets were everywhere in this place. I saw these amazing things that helped America become an international space power, and I have no doubt it shaped my own views of what was possible for humans.

I mean, we had magic, but *we'd* never been to the moon.

But it was an experience my sisters, who were homeschooled so they wouldn't stray too far from the coven, never got to have. Not until today.

If I'd been home, I would have had all three of my sisters here as children, I thought as we wandered into a small planetarium display.

Though maybe that wasn't fair.

Maybe Ayla never asked to go.

I frowned.

Kids shouldn't have to ask for something like—

Without warning, the hair on the back of my neck bristled.

I spun and saw a man in the entryway staring at my sisters.

None of my sisters noticed him. The girls were transfixed by a large, glowing map of our solar system on the planetarium's main display. Tiny red, blue, and green lights reflected in their eyes as they stared into the depths of the abyss. The air was still and quiet except for the low hum of the hydraulic projector cables.

Who was he?

The man was handsome and carried himself with confidence. He wore a brown tailored suit, with a crisp white shirt underneath. He was slightly disheveled, with wispy hair cut too long and an unshaven face, but overall he projected an air of professional and physical grace.

I was about to say something to my sisters, but then the tall man turned around and looked me in the eye. He pointed at my sisters and then glared at me once again before walking away

"Wait here," I told them and took off after him, pulling my glove off as I went. "And I mean it. Don't move."

I needed only to introduce myself, shake his hand, and get a read on him. Then I'd know his intentions, maybe even his identity.

The man strode through the Space Center, and I hurried to keep up. He wasn't going in a pattern; he just walked quickly and with purpose, like he was going to an appointment. He cut around families looking at the displays, and he didn't slow until his phone rang.

I maneuvered close enough so I could listen in.

"...the Decanus caught me watching them, so I had to go."

I ducked behind an educational booth.

"I don't know what they're doing, but they're acting like run of the mill tourists, and they're pretty insistent on the whole act." He paused. "Yes. It's definitely her. She's still wearing her military uniform, and there are four of them. I'm sure it's them." He chuckled. "Maybe she can't let go, I don't know. I appreciate you letting me know." A pause. "I will."

He hung up and kept walking.

There was no way I could just walk up to the guy, introduce myself, and extend my hand now, I thought. I watched him reach the exit and step outside.

Finally, I turned on my heel and made my way back toward the planetarium. Sticking close to my sisters suddenly became way more important.

I didn't want Archie to be correct, but despite my constant teasing, the bird was right more than he was wrong. Something strange was going on here—and all initial indications pointed to paranormal drama on the Space Coast.

Only a paranormal would know all four of us on sight, my previous rank, and that my uniform was military.

I was halfway back to the planetarium when I noticed my three sisters approaching me. I reinserted my hand into my glove and forced a smile.

"What was that about?" Ami asked me. Her narrowed eyes gave her a condescending look. She raised an eyebrow and crossed her arms over her chest.

"Nothing."

"Nothing, huh?" If you took out a dictionary and looked up suspicious, you would have found a picture of Ami's face. "You were chasing a guy. Who was he?"

"Just some guy," I said.

"A guy you've never seen before?" Althea asked. "Or one you've seen before?"

I forced a laugh. "Guys, come on."

"Don't treat us like idiots, Astra," Ami said. "We're not children you have to protect. Who was he?"

I raised my hands. "Look, I honestly don't know."

"But?" Ayla asked.

The worst part about lying is that the truth is always right there, hanging around in the center of your thoughts. No matter what you do, it's always there, staring at you and mocking you and giving off an energy that the intuitive can sense.

I didn't want to have this conversation in the Kennedy Space Center, but my sisters were not so easy to fool anymore.

I paused and looked toward the exit, then back at my three suspicious sisters. "But he knew who we were, he was watching us, and he doesn't think we're here for vacation. And since I don't know what's going on, we're not discussing it here."

* * *

WE SLUMPED into the lobby of the condo, exhausted from our hasty return from the Space Center. We had been a little nervous outside in public, despite the fact that we were surrounded by hundreds of other people. We were just relieved to be back in safety, where we didn't have to be so cautious of anyone watching us.

At least, I thought it was safe.

Charles, the ever-present doorman, nodded as

we returned and raced to open the elevator for us. "Did you enjoy your day at the Space Center?" he asked cheerfully. "You were gone for much less time I expected."

Althea frowned. "Charles, who do you work for?"

I glared at her. "Althea."

"What?" she asked me. "It's just a question."

She was just a little blunt.

Not the way I would have handled it.

But I had to admit that she was correct in her question, and I was impressed that she realized it without any of us discussing it. We'd been followed, and the man who had followed us seemed to know exactly where we'd be. Aside from the four of us, only one other person knew we were going to the Kennedy Space Center today.

And that person was holding the elevator door open.

Charles smiled warmly.

And I mean it when I say it was a warm, seemingly genuine smile. The kind of smile that got into his eyes, that lit up his face and made him look ten years younger. It was the kind of smile that said Charles had been working as a doorman for a long time and was having a great time doing it. It was the kind of smile you'd see on someone who was overjoyed.

And yet…I didn't buy it for a second.

"Mr. Remington and all of the other managers for the complex are gone for the week," he said. "I'm in charge of this building right now while they're gone."

"They're all gone the week that we're here?" Ami asked. "Isn't that kind of a weird coincidence?"

Charles's smile widened, and then he winked. "I don't know what you mean," he repeated. "Now, if you'll excuse me, I have a lot of work to do."

He stepped back, and the elevator door slid closed.

Ami's eyes blazed with curiosity, and she stared at the closed doors intently. Althea's eyes darkened, and her gaze shifted to the floor. Ayla was motionless, her pupils dilated and her gaze fixed on Ami.

"Well," Althea said, looking up. "I guess we're not on vacation."

CHAPTER FOUR

*T*he four of us stormed into the condo as if on a mission.

Which, technically, I guess we kind of were.

Ami snatched her tarot cards from her brown leather purse with a look of eager anticipation. She raced across the polished marble floor of the condo, the heels of her flat shoes clicking with each hurried step.

Ayla's nose flared, and she breathed deeply. She rubbed her arms as she turned in circles, examining the walls with a practiced eye as if looking for ghostly evidence of spirits long gone. "It's like the whole place has been scrubbed clean," she murmured to herself.

I looked around Amelia's condo, finally concerned that her absence wasn't just our cousin leaving to do something else. With the strangeness of the entire building, the suspiciously friendly Charles, and the key thrown through the magical cauldron without explanation, it was beginning to appear that Amelia was clearly concealing something.

Or entangled in something.

Or the victim of something.

But what exactly?

"I need to mix up protection potions," Althea told me as we followed the other two in. Eyeing me up and down, she asked, "Planning on taking those gloves off any time soon and, you know, *doing* anything?" Althea smirked. "And yes, I do mean that figuratively and literally."

I scowled at her, yanked off the gloves, and tossed them to her. I didn't know who was more surprised, her or me.

She handed them back. "Jeez, Astra, I was just joking."

My jaw stiffened, and my eyes narrowed dangerously as I replaced my gloves. "You know, I was the one who noticed someone following us around the Space Center. While the three of you were transfixed by blinking lights, I was trying to figure out what was going on. So, you know, I don't appreciate the snide—and inaccurate—statement that I'm doing nothing."

"Lighten up, big sister. I really was just teasing you," Althea responded, her voice low.

I shot her a look, daring her to say another word.

"No fighting." Ami dropped a large, unwieldy deck of tarot cards onto the polished wooden table. They sprawled out in a fan-like pattern, with the skull decorations on their backs leering up at us like smug know-it-alls. She slowly gathered them back into a pile, shuffled, and nodded to herself. "Okay, I need to draw the cards," she announced with authority, "and I don't want your snippy energy affecting the reading. So put it in your pocket, ladies."

"What snippy energy?" I retorted, my hands on my hips. Ami's eyes raised, and she looked at me steadily. "What? What now?" She continued staring. "I swear, you move at a snail's pace. If you're done with the lecture, maybe we can get down to business?" I held my hand out toward the cards.

"Nope, no snippy energy here," Ayla breathed.

Ami glanced at Ayla and cracked a smile, then nodded. Her eyes dropped and focused on the deck. "Okay, so, the first thing I need to see is if the cards will give us some indication as to where, or how, Amelia is. Is she safe," she mused, "or is she in trouble? If she's in trouble, we'll follow that thread."

"Not trying to derail this, but wouldn't it be faster for Astra to just read the key?" Althea asked. Her hair fell into her eyes, and she distractedly pushed it away. "Obviously, Amelia sent it to us for a reason, and we still don't know what it represents. Shouldn't we start there?"

"It'd be faster to just go downstairs and ask Charles outright what the heck is happening," Ayla responded, her eyebrow raised. "But we have no idea what's going on, and this whole building is all magicked up. I wouldn't be surprised if that key was, too. We need more information before we start opening up to things."

"Ayla's right." Ami's eyes drifted up briefly from the deck of cards on the table. "Before we go poking around in things we know nothing about, we should let the cards give us some indication—if they can—of what we're dealing with here." She flipped over cards in a particular cross-like pattern. "We might be able to get some indication..." Ami's voice trailed off and her eyebrows knotted. "Oh. Oh no."

I could see a few cards Ami had laid out on the table vaguely, but I felt them more than saw them. The disturbing energy of the cards Ami flipped over felt…dark. I couldn't quite make out what they were, but what they portended seemed ominous.

My stomach churned.

Ami paused and took a long, deep breath. She closed her eyes and exhaled. She opened her eyes and nodded. She mouthed words silently as if in prayer over the messages from the universe.

"Well?" I asked, unable to avoid sounding impatient.

"I think…" Ami said, her voice soft. "I think this is really bad, guys." She pushed a card out at me. "See?"

I looked down at the card, trying to suppress a shudder.

The image depicted a woman drowning, her hair wrapped tightly around her neck in a noose of death, while a giant serpent circled her and roared in triumph.

The words at the bottom of the card read "The Death Card."

"You're not saying you think Amelia's dead," I argued, unwilling to accept that the cards could be that literal. "If I've heard it once, I've heard it a thousand times. The humans get all paranoid about the Death card, but the Death card doesn't mean death. It means rebirth or something." I looked at Ami. "Right?"

Ami flipped a few more cards out and then turned her gaze toward me again. Her eyes were intent, like she was weighing the words she was about to say. "You're right. That's what we tell humans. We tell them the Death card doesn't mean death. That's what we tell them." She paused. "Except sometimes, it *does* mean death."

"Are you sure?"

"I'm never a hundred percent sure. The cards are never that exact or definitive. There is an art to this, even with my intuition and natural seer power," Ami admitted. "And yes, at first, I thought maybe it was a card about symbolism, representing a traumatic event. But this…this is too literal, Astra," she said, her voice trailing off. "The additional cards I pulled indicate this isn't metaphorical at all. Water. New beginnings."

"Well, what do they tell you?" I asked. "Exactly?"

"Just what I said. For sure? Just that she's dead. I don't know," Ami responded, her face pained. "They won't tell me any more."

Ayla's face paled. "They stopped talking to you?"

"They don't really *talk*, but yes," Ami nodded. "Like I said, I'm not getting any more than that. Just a clear feeling that she's already passed on, and it has to do with water."

* * *

I DON'T KNOW how long we stood there mourning a cousin we hadn't seen in years and barely knew, but she was family.

She was one of us.

And she was probably dead.

I stared at the cards that Ami had laid out across the table. The Death card, the Water card, crossed by the Ace of Cups. The Ace of Cups represented new beginnings, and the Death card… well, according to Ami, it represented death.

I shivered.

Amelia was dead.

I cursed myself for not doing something sooner. Had I been more suspicious of the circumstances, maybe I would have realized how serious the danger was. I should have known. I should have sensed something was off.

But then again, what danger?

A single key?

A strange conversation on the phone with a cousin I didn't know well?

A snotty neighbor?

"Why would she be in the water?" Althea asked, her eyes pained. "Why would she be surrounded by water?"

Archie fluttered into view just off the back patio. "You guys should see what's going on down by the beach! Cop cars and people all staring!" he said as he flew in and perched on the edge of the tabletop. "With all the excitement, the frogs are hiding, so I came back."

Althea, Ami, and I exchanged a glance, but Ayla was the first to speak. "I don't believe in coincidences," she said, her voice wavering. "How much do you want to bet that Amelia's body was discovered on the beach today?"

Archie looked startled. "Amelia's body? Your cousin?" He fluttered on the edge of the table and stared at me. "Why do you think it's your cousin?"

"Because Ami just told us she knows Amelia is dead," Ayla replied, her eyes steely. "A psychic reading of the cards."

He craned his neck down, his beak open. "Oh!

I'm sorry, I didn't realize—" He looked up at us again. "Is there anything I can do?"

"This is so *weird*," Althea said, her voice hard. "What are the odds that Amelia dies, and then her body turns up on the beach in the same week that we visit, in the same week that the managers of this building are away?"

"I told you," Ayla said. "I don't believe in coincidences."

Archie's eyes popped open even further. "You think someone killed her?"

"If they did, someone might be trying to frame us," Ayla admitted. "Think about it. We show up, and a day later, she's dead?"

"We don't know when she died," Ami pointed out.

"We know she was alive two days ago." Althea pointed toward me. "Astra and Mom talked to her."

"I really want to know what's going on down on that beach," My expression was grim as I walked toward the patio. "But if any of us go down there, we're just going to look suspicious to the police."

"Who will probably be here any minute," Ami added, following me outside.

"I'll do a flyover of the beach, see what I can

see," Archie offered, skittering toward the ledge. "But I'm not sure what I can do to help. From up there, all I'll be able to see is ant-like people."

"I think you should concentrate your efforts on anyone the police might be talking to that don't look like other officers. And anyone watching a little *too* closely," Althea said, her tone matter-of-fact. "Just watch closely, and try to keep an eye out for any humans that might have spotted her body."

"Should I take note of any paranormals?" Archie asked.

I nodded. "If you can tell that someone's a paranormal, yes."

Archie looked at me as if I'd just insulted him. His neck feathers puffed out, and he let loose with a shrill chirp. "I'm not just any bird, you know. I can tell," he snapped. "It's the same way I know that you're not a bird." He leaned forward and pointed his beak at me. "If I can tell! Of all the insulting—"

The owl launched himself off the ledge and swooped down to the beach below while continuing to complain about my lack of respect.

"I've been thinking," Ami said as the four of us stood against the railing and watched the police on the beach from afar. "Why does a condo building with six tenants need multiple managers?"

"Honestly, Ami, I feel like we're way past that question," Althea told her.

Ayla frowned. "I don't think we're past it," she said. "If we were past it, we'd have an answer to it. And we don't."

The ocean glistened in the afternoon sun. The beach was such an impossibly long stretch of sand with rolling dunes and an endless expanse of surf. The sun was white-hot in the center of a sky so blue it looked like a master painter had just applied the last coat of color. The wind was warm on my skin. The breeze felt pleasant.

Everything seemed so peaceful.

"This would have been a great vacation," Ami observed sadly. "You know, I was looking forward to getting to know Amelia. I remember her from when we were younger. She was always so quiet at the family reunions, but from what I can remember, she seemed sweet." Ami turned toward Ayla. "Have you seen her? Her ghost, I mean?"

Ayla shook her head. "If I did, I wouldn't know it. No one's approached me. But I don't remember her very well. I was really young the last time I saw her, and there are no photographs in the condo. So I don't even know if I'd recognize her, to be honest." Ayla squinted toward the beach. "I don't see any ghosts down there at all."

We watched silently as the police did their work.

"For now, maybe we should all go back inside," I told them. "I'm afraid we're going to draw suspicion if we stay out here too long."

Just as I was turning, I saw a head pop up far out in the ocean.

If the mermaid's appearance hadn't been so striking, I never would have spotted her. Her hair was long and silver, streaming behind her in the water. Her skin was the color of pearl, her eyes a deep, dark blue, and they caught the light so intensely that they appeared to glow. She looked up at the sky, silently staring as she was buoyed in the ocean.

"Look!"

"What is that?" Ayla gasped.

"That's a mermaid," I whispered, as if saying it too loud would cause the creature to disappear.

"Oh, come on. There aren't any mermaids," Ami said, shaking her head.

"There are," I told her. "They're a type of

paranormal. A type of shapeshifter." I stared. "I think she's watching what's going on."

"I thought she might be." The voice came from the top of the building. We looked up and saw the owl flying toward the railing. "The police haven't noticed her at all, and I didn't want to fly down and draw attention to her."

"Archie, what do you think she's doing?"

The mermaid suddenly turned her head and looked up at us.

We all ducked down, except for the owl, who didn't seem concerned. Archie looked at me weirdly. "Are you people seriously afraid of a fish-woman a quarter mile out to sea?"

"A quarter mile?" Ami repeated.

Archie shrugged. "Maybe a little less? I can't tell from here." He hopped to the top of the railing. "You mean to tell me you're not going to talk with her?"

"Not at the moment," I told him.

"Why? Do you think she knows what happened to Amelia?" Althea asked.

Archie shrugged. "She was watching. She seemed to be interested." The owl took off again and flew toward the mermaid.

"Wait!" I tried to grab for him, but I was too slow.

I'm not sure if it was because of Archie's approach or because she had seen enough, but the mermaid slid under the water before the owl got halfway there. Archie flew over the location where she'd been bobbing, but she was nowhere to be found.

"I hope he knows not to come back for a bit," I muttered.

"Why?"

"They're loading Amelia up into the coroner's van," I told Ayla, pointing. "Those cops are going to be here any minute."

* * *

A BUZZER on the wall of the lobby rang loudly, and I pushed the button with a sense of dread. "Yes?"

"Ms. Arden, it's Charles in the lobby. There are two detectives down here to speak to you." Charles spoke with a smooth voice like he did this kind of thing every day.

"Okay, send them up," I replied.

There was a brief pause from his end as he asked something of the two detectives. His voice changed as he spoke again to me, his tone more firm. "Well, now, we don't really want to do that, do we? The apartment isn't a crime scene, and you don't have to let them in without a warrant—which I have asked for, and they don't have." The doorman sounded like he was completely aware of his rights—and mine—and confident in his position.

I blinked.

Who the heck was this guy, anyway?

"Are you a lawyer, Charles?"

"Me? Oh, goodness, no. Just a full-service doorman." He cleared his throat. "The way I see it? You could give the detectives what they want by letting them in, or you can try to force them to return with a warrant. On the one hand, you might be able to stall them before they get the warrant—or they might not get one at all—and on the other hand, they might get one. In which case, you've just delayed the inevitable. But of course, it's entirely up to you."

"Right," I said. "Thanks, Charles. That's... helpful." I paused. "I think."

"I'm sorry," he said, sounding truly apologetic. "I'm afraid I have no idea what you mean. I'm just following the protocol. Now, would you still like me to send them up?"

"No, I'll be right down," I told him and released the button.

Althea, Ami, and Ayla moved to stand in a small huddle near the elevator.

"I don't think we should split up," Ayla said to me.

"I disagree. You three stay here."

"Don't be silly," Ami said. "We'll go with you."

"Not a good idea." I shook my head. "We don't know what's going on here yet, and I do have the benefit of working for a police department. Besides, whatever Charles's role is in all this, it sounds like he won't let the police up here without a warrant, anyway."

Even though I hadn't pressed the button, the elevator dinged, and the doors slid open. We glanced at each other.

"That was creepy," Ayla muttered.

"I think Astra's right," Althea said finally. "Let's stay here, but you be careful."

"I will."

During the brief elevator ride, there was an eerie silence. Whatever I said to the detectives, I wouldn't be of help to Amelia, and I could cause problems for us. I didn't know enough about Amelia's life to speculate on her death, and what I did know about my cousin wasn't information I could volunteer to human police.

I just hoped that I wouldn't have to say too much during the meeting.

The elevator doors opened. I stepped out into the lobby and immediately spotted a tall woman in a dark business suit eyeing me with a hard expression. Her hair was cut short and styled in a no-nonsense bob, and her shoes were sensible pumps. Black Ray-Ban sunglasses perched on her head, and in her right hand, she held her badge, dangling on its chain.

Before she could speak, a man with salt and pepper hair, a deep tan, and a black mustache that ran all the way to his cheekbones stepped up beside her. His eyes were startlingly pale blue and they watched me with a piercing gaze that conveyed an intense annoyance. "It's about time," the man said.

This was starting off well.

"I'm sorry," I told him. "I was in the middle of something. What can I do for you?"

"In the middle of something, huh?" he demanded roughly. "And what exactly was that?"

"Marcus," his partner said sharply.

He turned his gaze from me back to his partner with narrowed eyes. Her eyes caught his and held them, like a snake watching its prey.

"Ms. Arden?" the woman asked, turning back toward me.

Marcus continued to stare at her.

I nodded.

"I'm Detective Rebecca Harris," she said. "This is my partner, Detective Saul Marcus. I'm sorry to tell you this, but we found your cousin's body on the beach."

CHAPTER FIVE

"What happened?" Because it was early in their investigation, I assumed I knew at least as much as they did when I asked the question, but not asking would have raised suspicions.

Detective Harris informed me they had no idea what had occurred but that they were looking into it. "Do you have contact information for her parents or closest next of kin?" she asked.

I shook my head. "Her parents are no longer with us, Detective. As far as I'm aware, we're her closest family, but I'll give my mother a call and see if there's anyone we need to inform."

"Thank you." Detective Harris turned to face

Charles, who was standing at attention behind his desk, clearly listening in. "At this point, we don't know if there was any foul play or not, but that's what we're trying to find out. Mr. Undine, when was the last time you saw Ms. Arden—Amelia Arden?"

"She was here yesterday morning," Charles said. "I wished her a good morning, we spoke briefly, and then she left about nine in the morning. In a blue bathing suit with a silver sarong and blue sandals." I was so taken with the doorman's swift delivery of information I didn't notice Detective Harris had used his surname.

Her bobbed haircut bounced as she nodded. "Thank you. What did you two discuss? Did she say anything about where she might be going after that?"

Charles ran his hand through his hair, paused, and then said, "Well, she was in a rush, you know. But she mentioned something about going out on the water." He turned toward the door and peered at the parking lot, his eyes glassy and faraway. "And, of course, she let me know that her cousins would be coming from Forkbridge to visit later that day so I could prepare the key cards."

"And how did she seem?" Detective Harris asked. "Was she her normal self?"

"Well—" Charles hesitated as if thinking back. "Yes, she seemed just fine. As far as I could tell. Nothing unusual. She didn't seem upset or agitated. Maybe a bit quieter than usual."

Detective Harris nodded and looked toward the door. She seemed as if she wanted to go outside and check something, but then she looked down at her notes. "Mr. Undine," she said, "did Amelia have any distinguishing features?"

That time caught my attention.

Mr. *Undine*? Did she say undine?

I stared at Charles.

Undines (or Ondines) are water-related elemental spirits. The term was coined by Theophrastus von Hohenheim—also known as Paracelsus, a Swiss Renaissance alchemist, and physician. His posthumously published *Book on Nymphs, Sylphs, Pygmies, and Salamanders, and on the Other Spirits* stood right beside other tomes on chemistry and medicine like *The Great Surgery Book*.

He was an interesting guy, that Paracelsus.

But he was a human—and therefore wrong about paranormals in many respects.

Many, *many* respects.

He was not wrong, though, about their existence.

"Distinguishing features?" Charles asked. "Oh. You mean scars, or tattoos, or—"

"Or birthmarks. Anything like that."

"Not that I recall." Charles Undine's eyes dropped down, and he suddenly examined his fingernails.

"You don't recall? Really? Ms. Arden had a fairly prominent tattoo."

Charles looked up distractedly. "I beg your pardon?"

Detective Harris stared at Charles intently. "A tattoo. You said she was in a bathing suit. Surely you saw it. Your tenant has a tattoo. On her left shoulder."

"Does she?" he asked calmly. "Fascinating. What does it look like?"

Detective Marcus's eyes were glued to my face as Detective Harris told Charles, "It's a crescent moon with a star inside of it."

The mention of a star inside anything, even something as insignificant as a tattoo, made me tense. The star power of Astraea (which I possessed as a gift from the goddess Athena) was not widely known to exist. Even those in the paranormal world who knew I had some strange, one-of-a-kind witch power had no idea what it was or where it had come from.

The doorman wore a contemplative expression as though he was considering a response. "Interesting. What color is the moon?" he asked casually.

Detective Harris looked at her notes. "Pink."

She waited for a response, but no one said a word.

After a few more moments of silence, Detective Harris glanced at her notes and said, "Anyway, as I mentioned, it's possible that we're dealing with a run of the mill drowning. But we certainly can't rule out foul play. While we're here, Ms. Arden—Mr. Undine mentioned that you and your sisters never even saw your cousin. Is that true?"

"Yes. We arrived after she left the condo yesterday."

"Really?" Detective Harris looked at me with a cautious glance. "That's very curious, don't you think?"

There was a lot about this situation that was curious.

Most of which I wasn't planning on mentioning to the human.

Detective Harris looked at me for a moment before saying slowly, "Well then, I think we're done here. If you think of anything else, anything at all, please call." She handed me her card, then turned back to Charles. "And you, if you remember anything else that seems odd, please don't hesitate to call us."

She stepped toward the door, then paused to take one last look at Charles. Her gaze darted back and forth before returning to me. "Are you sure I can't take a look around Amelia's apartment?"

"I need to let my sisters know what happened to Amelia, and I'd like to do that without an audience. It also doesn't seem like you know whether a crime has been committed yet or not. If you think there has been, feel free to give me a call. For now, I think we'd prefer to maintain Amelia's privacy." I tilted my head. "We'd also like some space to mourn."

"The cousin you haven't seen since you were a child?" Detective Marcus's question was delivered in a raspy, accusatory tone. He licked his lips and looked me in the eyes. "You need to mourn someone you barely knew?"

"We were family, Detective Marcus," I told him. "That counts for something."

"Does it?" he sneered. His eyes narrowed into dark slits beneath a heavy brow that hung over his eyes like a shelf. He reminded me of a walrus, with fleshy folds hanging around his face and neck. "When you don't know anything about the person you're mourning?"

"We know enough," I responded quietly.

The man turned and twisted the polished brass knob. "By the way, do you have a tattoo?" he asked.

"That's none of your business."

He chuckled to himself.

The two detectives pushed open the glass doors and were gone.

* * *

CHARLES LEFT his post behind the marble desk when the detectives left. In less than a second, he was in front of me, his hand on my exposed shoulder. "Miss Arden, I'm so terribly sorry," he said as he placed his hand on my back. "Your cousin was a wonderful girl."

I stepped away from the man's touch just as the image of water churned my mind. "You're an undine."

As Charles blinked, all the fish in the massive lobby aquariums stopped swimming and turned to follow my movement with their black eyes. Then they reoriented themselves to stare at the doorman. With a sigh, he ran his hand lovingly over one window of the large tank.

"Yes, I am."

I felt the beady eyes of dozens of fish staring at me once more as if waiting to see what I would do with this information. "Why didn't you tell me?"

"It's not something I go around shouting at people. Obviously." He sat down at his desk, leaned back, and gestured toward a second chair. "Miss Arden, before you begin pelting me with questions, I'd like to apologize again for the death of your cousin. The poor girl had a profound impact on everyone in this place and the ocean itself."

Profound, huh?

That could be a good thing or a bad thing. I wasn't sure which underlying message Charles was trying to convey based on his tone. My eyes drifted to the skinny goldfish that was nibbling on a piece of seaweed. His speech, though, was tinged with a trepidation he couldn't quite hide.

I moved around the reception area and took the seat offered. "What do you mean she had a profound impact?" The fish in the tanks turned away from me and resumed their swimming—though much more slowly than before.

"Most people loved her. She was a delight to be around." He pulled his necktie loose and took a deep breath. "She was also in high demand."

"For?"

"Her skills."

"Her skills."

His expression grew confused. "Yes, her skills."

It was difficult to elicit information from a paranormal being. We were creatures of self-preservation—and some of us rarely spoke the truth unless it was wrapped in a truth spell. I wasn't sure about undines. I knew of them but had never dealt with them before.

To be honest, it's no surprise we paranormals are a little difficult—if humans weren't after us, the Witches' Council was. That had been the case for hundreds of years. Other than what we created for ourselves, paranormals had little privacy and security.

To combat that, the paranormal world was, by nature, a secretive place.

"What kind of skills?"

His clean-shaven face wrinkled at the edges as if he were trying to hide his thoughts. I waited for him to decide what story he would tell me, and the silence dragged on as we watched one another.

Finally, he leaned forward and said, "She is—was—a certified Hex Master."

Amelia a *Hex Master*?

It was hard to believe.

A hex is a negative witchcraft spell that can cause anything from great misfortune to serious physical harm. A hex, also known as a jinx, a curse, or the whammy, is anything a witch throws at someone that causes bad things to happen to them.

Yes, almost any witch can learn to hex just like any human can learn to bake a loaf of bread from a video on the internet. Hexing? Not that hard.

But if Amelia's special talent was Hex Master level whammies, it meant she could curse others to cause problems and harm while avoiding the normal consequences of such malicious behavior. Her hexes would be untraceable and have no consequences for her or anyone else.

Well, other than the poor sod she hexed.

People—humans, witches, other paranormals

—would pay top dollar to hire out the kind of untraceable damage a Hex Master could do.

"There are no certified Hex Masters anymore," I told Charles. "The Hex Master Guild was disbanded at the same time the Ministry of Arcane Fugitives was."

Charles cocked a dubious eyebrow. "It's ironic that you say that while dressed in your Decanus uniform. And with a straight face, no less. Are you and your legionaries relaxing on a beach somewhere enjoying your *retirement?*" the undine asked me. "Have you turned in all the magical objects you stuffed in your duffel bags on your way out the door? Because I've heard otherwise."

Well.

Mr. Undine certainly seemed to know a lot.

I stared at Charles, my gloved fingertips steepled.

"Am I wrong?" the doorman asked.

I suddenly leaned forward and planted my elbows on my knees. "Okay, before we get too far into this—even though it has exactly nothing to do with Amelia—you answer a few questions for me. What is this place? Is everyone in this building a paranormal? Is this one of those hidden enclaves the Witches' Council was so paranoid about? And if so, what's the purpose of it?"

His eyes glittered with amusement. "So many questions for a retired soldier."

I raised an eyebrow. "So few answers."

Charles raised his eyebrows. "You think I'm going to answer all those questions?"

"Yep."

"Why?"

"Because you let my sisters and me into the building," I told him. "Because you kept the detectives at bay, because you stood between them and a search of Amelia's apartment. I don't know that I can trust what you say. I'll admit that. I don't know what's going on here." I pointed. "But you're an undine. I know that if you thought I was a threat, I probably would have drowned in a toilet by now."

"Oh, for Atlantis's sake. Just tell her," a small voice gurgled. "Maybe they're on our side for a change."

* * *

I JUMPED up and looked around the lobby, but no one was there.

"Athena and Poseidon may have fought over

Athens, but they haven't busted heads for years now," a high-pitched voice babbled with a splash. "We can probably trust her. We trusted Amelia. Maybe we can trust her. If not, the toilet drowning is still an option."

"Who's here?" I asked. "Who's saying that?"

Quiet burbled laughter erupted from all sides.

I looked around and saw nothing but fluttering fish—

Oh, come on.

"No," I said out loud as I examined the tank.

More water-logged laughter.

"You must be kidding me," I whispered as beady eyes stared back at me from the brightly colored fish tank. "They can all talk? All of them?"

The fish continued to stare and whisper among themselves.

"Are you sure?" Charles asked, gazing toward the aquarium.

The aquatic inhabitants of the two large tanks looked at me through the thick glass. Their irises glistened ominously, their eyes onyx black. Just over Charles's shoulder, my gaze was drawn to the eyes of a large Filefish. His expression seemed to shift, a constant blinking and flurried movement of worry.

"I'll take your silence as confirmation," the

undine said. "This is an undine clan enclave. One of many. We're a closely held secret of the supernatural world, though no doubt the Council is well aware of us—and we would like to remain that way."

"Why the secrecy?" I asked.

"Because we're nothing like what most people think we are," he said with a smile. "We're nothing like the stories told about us over the centuries."

"And because most of us taste good poached," a small voice murmured.

"Okay, I'll bite. What are you?" I asked.

"A peace-loving people. This is our territory."

"Well," I said with a laugh. "Not people, exactly."

"Rude," a high-pitched burble squeaked.

"Yes, all of them, a peace-loving people," Charles repeated as he leaned forward and looked at me with his hands clasped. "From the little brown ones to that magnificent dolphin." He pointed toward a bright green fish with bulging eyes. "For three miles around this place in every direction, there's a truce. No one eats anyone else."

Some of the fish in the tank moved away from the glass and inspected the marble columns as if they'd grown bored with the conversation. Several started nibbling at sea urchin shells on the bottom.

"Why here?" I asked. "And why would you want to be in tanks instead of in the ocean?"

"This is a hospital, you dolt," a small green fish burbled. "We're hurt, and we needed to heal somewhere we wouldn't get attacked by real fish or fished by the idiot humans." The fish swam up to the waterline and splashed furiously. "No one would choose to live like this. Obviously. I mean, *obviously*."

"I would," a little brown one said. "No one tries to eat me in here."

"You're such a wuss, Zedbid," another fish snapped. "I should eat you."

"Shut up, Nij!"

"Get your own tank," Nij snapped back as he swam away.

"Zedbid is right, though," a kingfish said as it swam up along the bottom of the tank closest to where Charles sat. He—or she—looked out at me. "It is why we gave an apartment to your cousin. The fishermen that follow the rules? They are easily avoided. The gill nets?" The fish shook in fear. "Even for intelligent creatures like us, gill nets are deadly."

I frowned. "What are gill nets?"

The fish flapped in the water and quickly turned around, swimming to the other side of the tank. "I don't even want to hear about it. You tell her, Charles."

Charles lifted his hands. "Fishing nets. Mesh sizes are chosen so that fish can only get their heads through the netting and not their bodies. As the fish tries to back out of the net, their gills become entangled in the mesh. As the fish tries to free itself, it becomes increasingly more entangled."

My jaw dropped. "That's horrible."

Charles smiled briefly as if my horror pleased him. "They're very effective. They're also illegal in many places around the world because of how destructive they are. Including Florida."

"If they're illegal, why are they—" I restrained myself from asking a stupid question when the answer was that bad people who can get away with breaking the law will be tempted to do so regardless of who they hurt. "Sorry. Destructive how?"

"It's hard to take the fish out of the nets, so they're left to die whether they were meant to be caught or not. Sea turtles encountering a gill net can quickly become entangled around their head or flippers as they try to escape."

"That's awful."

"Not even as bad as drift nets," Charles told me ominously. "Gill nets work as a swaying wall of death that entangles every animal, large or small, that pushes against their folds if they are not hung stiffly–and *all* fishers know how to make them hang loosely. Even though they are not supposed to, many do. Marine mammals entangled in set gill nets can drown while those entangled in drift gill nets can drag gear for miles as they migrate and forage, leading to extreme fatigue."

I shuddered as the undine explained the damage, horrified at the idea of being trapped like that. "Okay, let's back up a second. I agree. These things are horrible. I still don't understand what this has to do with Amelia," I told Charles. I looked politely at the fish tanks and nodded, even though I felt ridiculous. "Amelia's a witch, not an undine."

"We just told you. Amelia was a Hex Master," a fish told me.

"We brought her in to hex the fishermen using the gill nets, obviously," another added. "We couldn't depend on anyone else to address the growing problem, illegal as it is. So we decided to take a stand."

"We didn't take a stand," Nij laughed. "We decided to destroy the murderous jerks, so we could swim in the ocean like we are meant to do without being worried something's going to kill us."

CHAPTER SIX

"Wait, wait," Ami interrupted me. She slowly lifted her hand to her face. Her long, thin fingers hooked over the edge of her thin lips, pulling them down and resting against her chin. "You're telling me you met a talking fish?"

Althea and Ayla watch me intently. Not a single blink, twitch, or movement. The room is silent. They just watch, waiting for the punchline to the joke.

"More than one." I nodded. "I don't know whether I can trust Charles completely, but I heard the fish. His story adds up." Ayla looked thoughtful while Ami and Althea remained agog. "The fish people gave Amelia this apartment in exchange for helping them with their gill net issues."

"Undines," Ayla corrected, her eyes narrowing. "They're a paranormal species. Don't call them fish people. That's not respectful."

"I'm not trying to be disrespectful. They are fish people. They are fish that can transform into human-looking people and back again. So, fish people." Ayla frowned slightly. "In fact, when I implied they weren't people, they got a little defensive."

"Did Charles have any idea what happened to Amelia?"

I shook my head. "But he did tell me what the key was for."

Crossing the condo, I pushed up against a large square painting of fish on the white wall. With a little pressure, the panel gave way and sprang out, revealing a mechanical-looking keyhole. Turning the key, the walls opposite me slowly rolled back, revealing massive fish tanks filled with darting and circling fish of all shapes and sizes. The room suddenly smelled densely of saltwater and faintly of algae.

"Holy mackerel," Althea breathed.

"Seriously? These four are supposed to find out who killed Amelia?" one squeaked. "I find that hard to believe. They can't even close their mouths."

"Are they old enough to magic? They don't look old enough to drink. Well, that one does," another said, turning its body toward me. "She looks way past her prime." I glared. "You think Charles has been smoking something? None of them are Hex Masters. I can tell from here. Say they find the killer. What are they gonna do? Sparkle 'em to death?"

"Amelia knew she was in danger," a large fish told the two smaller ones. "She decided to trust them with the key. She let them come here. We need to put our faith in the witches the universe brought us to—"

"The universe didn't bring them," another snapped. Ironically, it was a snapper—a light pinkish-orange fish with a small wound on the side of its face. "They came here for spring break, not because they cared about their cousin."

"Holy mackerel is right. I don't even know what to say here," Ami breathed, moving closer to get a better look at the fish as they swarmed about the bottom like a school of bloodthirsty piranhas. "Astra, did you see this? There's a hole in the back of the tank. There. Right there." I leaned forward. "Do you see that? Like a tunnel."

"Charles explained that this entire structure is essentially a fish tank." I pointed at the wall between the living room and dining room. "It's beneath the floor and between the walls of the entire structure. The condominiums conceal the tanks' existence, but each apartment has access to them through panels similar to this one."

"So they can swim anywhere? Visit anyone?" Althea asked.

"And hear everything, sweet cheeks," gruffed a giant fish with red scales and sails of yellow, black, and white. "These walls ain't that thick. You should hear the things we hear. If you heard the things we heard, you'd have heard it all."

"You're truly a wordsmith, Al," a white fish told him.

"Do fish even have ears?" Ami asked, her face confused. She leaned forward and examined the red-scaled fish closely. "I don't see any."

"They do," Althea nodded. "Hearing is accomplished through the sensory chambers of the inner ear. Each chamber contains an ear stone, and it's lined with sensory hair cells. The auditory nerves detect differences in vibrations between the ear stone and the sensory hair cells when sound vibrations pass through a fish."

"An ear stone?"

Althea nodded at Ami. "It's called an otolith. Look it up."

"Is she right?" a striped fish asked quietly. "I have rocks in my head?"

"How the in the Kraken's cave would I know?" a purple fish snapped. "Do you remember an internet-connected laptop on any of the sunken ships we visited?"

"Don't get snarky," the striped fish snapped back. "You sound like my ex-wife."

"Hey, you two," interrupted a small fish with a blue head, a white body, and a yellow fin poking out the top of its head like a Mohawk. "Amelia is dead. This is not the time."

"Oh, right. Right, right," the striped fish replied. "I'm sorry. This is just hard. Not that I knew her or anything, but the poor thing." He swam back and forth as if pacing. "Amelia wasn't in denial about the reality of our situation, at least. Even if half of these idiots didn't want to admit it, she knew trade and development were destroying our homes. Not to mention—"

"Don't you start about the casi—"

"But I know exactly what happened to her!" the striped fish cut off the small fish with a glare. "She was killed trying to stop the Cocoa Reef

Underwater Casino from opening. Why else would anyone kill her?"

* * *

THE FISH WERE helpful in directing us to Amelia's notes, daily planner, and record of hexing activities on the water. Althea also found newspaper articles about the proposed casino beneath Amelia's daily planner.

"It looks like the Firethorn Development Corporation heard about Lady Luck in Pompano Beach," Althea explained, her eyes scanning the articles quickly.

"Lady Luck?" Ayla asked.

"It's a sunken tanker, a diving attraction made up to look like a casino for sea life. It features three larger-than-life shark statues, a life-sized mermaid, and an interactive art exhibit that displays locally produced underwater artwork."

"So, an artificial reef," Ayla said.

"Right. But no gambling." Althea looked up. "It appears that's where the Firethorn Development Corporation felt they went wrong. They want to build an underwater casino three nautical miles out, in national waters."

"Don't you mean international waters?" Ami asked.

"Nope. It says national waters."

"Where's that?" I asked.

Althea looked up. "Florida state waters are from shore to three nautical miles on the Atlantic and from shore to nine nautical miles on the Gulf. In most places, federal waters extend from where state waters end out to about two hundred nautical miles or to where other country's waters begin. Depending."

"What's a nautical mile?" Ayla asked.

"A nautical mile is based on the circumference of the planet," I told her, remembering the lessons I was forced to take in the military. "If you cut the earth in half at the equator, you could pick up one of the halves and look at the equator as a circle, right? Now divide that circle into 360 degrees and understand each degree is sixty minutes. That's how they get a nautical mile. On earth, a minute of arc equals one nautical mile."

"Okay. And this matters because..." Ami looked around.

"It doesn't." Ayla shrugged. "I was just curious."

"Does it matter?" Ami looked at me.

"It does if you're going to get on a boat."

"It matters because a casino is supposed to be built in state waters. If it's in state waters, it should be regulated by Florida laws. But, if it's built in federal waters, in the national waters, it'll be regulated by federal laws," Althea explained.

I frowned. "That doesn't make any sense. Casinos are illegal in federal waters."

"That's right. According to the FDC, they have a team of lawyers who specialize in exploiting legal loopholes, and they found one," Althea nodded. "Look at this," she said, holding up the paper. "They're estimating the casino will support one thousand jobs in the area and bring in a billion dollars over the first ten years."

"Three miles offshore and underwater? I find that hard to believe," Ayla said. "And again, they can't build there, right?"

"They claim they bought the land from the federal government."

"But it's not land," Ami pointed out. "It's water."

"Right. I mean, that's what I would think. There's nothing to purchase," Althea agreed. "It's just a bunch of water."

"You know, there are a lot of man-made islands all over the world that operate outside of normal parameters," Ayla said. "The Uros people of Bolivia and Peru construct floating islands out of bunched totora reeds and build their villages on top of them. There are the crannogs in Scotland and Ireland. No Man's Land Fort in the Solent straight. Heck, there's Florida's Isola di Lolando in Biscayne Bay. That Sealand place. Joyxee Island in Mexico—that place is made out of bottles. Seriously."

We stared at Ayla.

"What? Althea isn't the only one that reads."

Althea smirked. "Had an interest in isolated islands, did we?"

"If you keep giving me that look, I might take the interest back up."

"Everything you've mentioned is above the waterline, though," Ami pointed out. "Building a casino underwater? That's a whole 'nother kettle of fish."

"Hey!" a black striped fish hollered.

"Sorry! Sorry," she called toward the tank. "Okay, so we have a casino going up out in the open ocean in national waters where casinos are illegal. That means they paid someone off or found a loophole to exploit that gets around federal regulations."

"I don't know how they're going to build it," I said. "But I can tell you there's something sketchy about the entire thing. If it was this easy, the east and west coasts would be ringed in underwater casinos three miles offshore."

"I'm inclined to agree with you," Althea nodded.

"And why did Amelia care about this thing?" I asked Althea.

"I don't know. I can't find any handwritten notes or anything. I don't know why she has all this stuff. I just know she does." Althea put the papers down on the table. "You do realize we started looking into this because a fish in a fish tank told us about it. It seems much more likely someone she hexed found out about her, knew the bad luck they were having would end with her death, and killed her."

"Does hexing work like that?" Ayla asked.

Ami nodded. "I don't know much about hexing, but I *do* know that. It's why hexers are so secretive about their talent. One, anyone starts having bad luck in their vicinity, people start to blame them for it. Two, killing them stops the bad luck in its tracks." Ami held up a spiral-bound book. "And Amelia was a busy bee. She hexed a lot of illegal fishermen, store owners that sold illegal gill nets, companies that bought illegal catch knowingly." She slapped the book on the table. "There must be a hundred people in here."

"Did Charles point you toward anything in particular?" Ayla asked me.

"The fish in the walls," I shrugged. "What this place is. What Amelia's true purpose was in this condominium. Beyond that? Not really."

"What about that woman?" Ayla asked, leaning forward.

"What woman?"

"The one that didn't want us to park where Amelia told us to."

"Yeah, what was that all about?" Ami wondered aloud. "Why was that so important?" She looked over at me. "If she lives here, she has to be a fish person, right?"

"Not necessarily," I told her. "Amelia wasn't."

"Fair point. But she has to have a role, right? What's her role? Charles oversees the place, Amelia hexed people that threatened the fish people." Ami raised an eyebrow. "So what or who is she?"

"And is anyone else here?" Althea asked. "Or is it just us, Charles, Parking Lot Karen, and a school of talking fish?"

"Let's not forget the guy following us around the Space Center," I pointed out. "Charles claimed

'Mr. Remington and all of the other managers' were gone this week. We know there are six condos, and we're in one. Charles is probably in one. Parking Lot Karen is probably in one," I said, counting on my hand. "That's three."

"Mr. Remington, who's gone this week, is probably in one," Ami added, nodding. "The phrase 'all of the other managers' implies at least two more."

"Unless they're all roommates or married."

"Ask the fish," Ayla suggested.

I held up a finger. "I'd like to point out that we don't know, at this point, that we can trust any of the fish. Or Charles. Or anyone in this building."

One fish made a sort of gurgling noise, and a few of the other fish murmured back to him. "You know, we're just a nonhuman species indigenous to fluid space," he called out. "No reason to insult us by implying we're liars."

"She wasn't insulting you. We just don't know you, and our cousin is dead after working for you. Sorry you're suspicious, but you're suspicious." Ayla shrugged and waved her hand at me. "Anyway, I understand that we don't know who we can trust, but once Archie returns from his all day buffet in the Florida swamp, we can have him peek in the windows to see if they told us the truth."

"He's checking out the crime scene," I told her defensively.

"He's eating his way back to the porch, and you know it," Ayla retorted.

* * *

I SWALLOWED my groan of annoyance as Ayla moved toward the fish tank to interrogate the fish. Yes, Archie could be a pain, and at times he wasn't entirely predictable, but Ayla previously turned into the girl from *The Exorcist* because she channeled our Aunt Gertrude.

It's not like my magic was the only magic that came with some weirdness and things that needed patience.

An uneasy silence swept the room as the three of us continued to absorb ourselves in Amelia's documents. The sound of my phone vibrating shattered the stillness. I looked at the screen. "Oh, crap," I muttered. "It's Mom."

"Are you sure?" Ami asked.

I stared at the phone and nodded.

"Just don't answer," Althea told me.

I looked up. "Has anyone told her about Amelia?"

Dead silence.

"You can't ignore her. You have to answer it," Ami told me.

The phone stopped ringing.

Five seconds later, it began again.

"Answer it, but Astra, you can't tell her what happened," Althea ordered. "She'd demand we come home immediately, or worse, show up here."

Ami looked at me and then took a deep breath. "I agree, but if you ever tell her I said that I will deny it."

I nodded.

"Hi, Mom! How are you doing?" I said into the phone, my tone light and cheerful. "Everything okay back in Forkbridge? Are you getting along with Aunt Gertrude okay? How's Aunt Gwennie? Do you miss us?"

"You're overdoing it!" Althea hissed.

She was right.

My chipper questions were met with a few seconds of silence. "Astra? Why are you answering your phone like that? Is there any reason you didn't answer your phone when I called the first time?" Mom asked. "My job as a mother and a high priestess would be a lot easier if you'd just pick up the phone occasionally and let me know you're okay, you know."

"Ma, we've been gone just one day. We're fine. And I'm talking like this because I'm just having such a wonderful time on vacation that I can't hide my happiness," I said with a breathy laugh. "But really, how are you?"

Althea and Ami's eyes widened. "She's going to come through that cauldron in, like, ten seconds. I'm sure of it," Ami whispered, her expression pained.

"How are you that bad at lying?" Ami whispered.

"She's not even lying, not really," Althea whispered, shaking her head. "She's just not telling Mom the whole truth."

"I heard that," Mom's voice sounded in my ear.

"Heard what?" I asked with a sinking feeling in my stomach.

"And for your information, I can tell when you're lying. All of your facial muscles tighten up, your voice gets a bit shrill, and you tell me how wonderful everything is instead of letting me know how you really feel. Now, what is Althea talking about? The whole truth about what?"

"I don't know what you're talking about," I

said with a smile while frantically waving at Althea and Ami to shut up. "That was just the television. We're having a great time in Cocoa Beach, Mom. It's gorgeous, the weather's great. Condo's awesome. We're safe and sound," I said in a calm, reassuring voice. "Everything's fine."

"Dear Goddess," Althea whispered. "Now you sound like a Stepford Witch."

"Are you all at the condo now?" she asked.

"We are," I agreed. "We went to the Space Center this morning, and we're all just tired. It was a lot to see, you know? In fact, Ma, I'm going to take a nap now. I'm really tired." I yawned exaggeratedly into the phone.

"No one else is there?" Mom asked.

I stopped my fake yawn and narrowed my eyes. "No, Mom, it's just us," I answered. "Why do you ask?"

"I just got a strange call from the police in Cocoa Beach about a dead body," Mom told me. "They didn't say who it was, but they said Amelia might have something to do with it, and they wanted me, as next of kin, to give them permission to search her condominium." Mom paused. "Is there something you want to tell me?"

"The police?" I repeated. "Nope. Nothing we need to tell you. That is strange. Did you give them permission to search the place?" My sisters froze, their eyes widening as if they couldn't believe what I had just said.

"Of course not. I told them to find Amelia and get her permission," Mom said, her voice dry. "I don't know why on earth they called me for permission."

"Just out of curiosity, Mom, who called you? Did you get a name?"

"I wrote it down; one second." I heard a drawer open and papers shuffle. "Yes, here it is. Detective Saul Marcus."

CHAPTER SEVEN

hirty-four years old, retired from the military, living at home, and now we're adding a dead cousin, corrupt detective, and talking fish to the mix.

My luck never ceased to amaze me.

Though, to be fair, I would take my luck over Amelia's any day.

I left the muggy room and stepped out onto the porch. Outside, the air was more humid than the condo, but a salty breeze from the ocean cooled my face.

I scanned the horizon.

Archie still wasn't back.

I needed Archie, and if he really was dive-bombing the amphibian population instead of

104 | LEANNE LEEDS

getting back here with a report of what the silver mermaid was doing, I would pluck his ear-flap feathers one by one.

I took a breath to steady my annoyance.

"I feel like you should just never claim anything is a vacation." Ayla stepped outside, pulling the sliding door closed behind her. Exhaling, she turned her face to the warm afternoon sun and basked in its light. "This happened with you and Emma, too. Maybe if you decided to take us all on a case, somebody could actually get a vacation for once."

"I don't believe the universe works like that," I told her, my hand shading the sun as I scanned the sparkling water. "Amelia's dead because Amelia got caught up in something shady, or uncovered something shady, or knew something that someone else didn't want anyone to know." No matter where I looked, Archie and the mermaid were nowhere to be found—but the police were still on the beach. "She's not dead because we decided to visit Cocoa Beach."

"How do you decide which reason is the reason?"

I tried to parse her question in my mind and failed. "I'm not sure I understand what you mean."

"Well, this whole building is one big hidden conspiracy of sick and injured undines, right? And Amelia was hexing people for them. So, she could have been killed because of something having to do with the building or the hexing. That's already two things," Ayla said, glancing up at me. "Then there's the casino the fish thinks she was killed over. Then there's the guy following us at the Space Center, so maybe she *was* killed because we showed up. And finally, there's whatever Detective Marcus is into, which could be any of the things I just named or something totally different."

"I'm going to assume he's into other things," I said, my gaze moving back to the beach. After a few moments, I turned back to Ayla. "He'd have to be. He's not a very good detective."

"Oh?" Ayla peeled off her flip-flops and took a swig from a bottle of lemonade. "How do you know? He barely talked."

"He told Mom his name. When you're doing something shady, you should be wise enough not to identify yourself. And there's the fact that he contacted Mom at all. He was attempting to get around laws he's required to follow. So, probably a bad cop. Or corrupt."

"How'd he get Mom's number, anyway?"

"We're Amelia's closest family, so Mom's probably her emergency contact for something."

Ayla held out the lemonade, and I took a sip as my gaze fell on a squad car pulling up to the beach. It was accompanied by a black Prius marked CORONER.

If that was the vehicle coming to transport Amelia's body, there seemed to be a significant (and rather suspicious) delay in their arrival—especially considering the spring heat.

"No ghosts here, by the way," Ayla told me in a hushed voice.

"None at all? Not a single one?"

Ayla's eyebrows rose.

"I do not doubt you, Ayla. I'm just clarifying. I thought you'd have spotted Amelia by now."

"Maybe I'm wrong about there being ghosts here, or maybe this place just doesn't have any," Ayla said, leaning against the railing. "There's definitely something very different about this building, so all I can say for sure is that I don't see any. What does that mean? No idea. To be honest, I expected Amelia to show up here, too. She knows I can communicate with her."

I turned back to scan the water when I noticed a second boat at the condo dock.

One that hadn't been there the day before.

"Ayla, look," I said, pointing. "Do you remember that second boat being there yesterday?" It was a small fishing boat, about twenty feet long, and it looked like it was in bad shape. The hull was weathered, and the paint was peeling. There was a tattered flag at the stern, but I couldn't make out the design. "You see it? That small one?"

Before she could answer, I saw movement on the fishing boat.

It was a man.

He was wearing a large straw hat, sunglasses and was dressed in a white shirt with blue jeans. He walked to the bow and then leaned over the side of the boat, the wind whipping the back of his shirt and the waves crashing against the hull. His eyes scanned through the water, and he tapped at his chin as if he was in deep thought.

It looked like he was watching something or watching *for* something.

"What's he doing?" Ayla whispered.

"I don't know. And you don't need to whisper. I don't think he can hear us."

He slowly paced back and forth along the deck. His posture was hunched over, and he kept his hands locked behind his back. Sometimes, he would stop, stretch his hand out to plunge it into the water, then slowly pull his hand out of the water and place something in the bucket at his feet. He stood there for a few moments, looking at what he had collected, and then continued pacing until he repeated the entire thing once more.

"Damn it, Archimedes," I muttered. "Where are you when I need you?"

"I'll get the binoculars I brought," Ayla said, and then she handed me her lemonade. "We can see what he's doing. Be right back."

I watched and waited.

Seconds later, an arm appeared from the corner of my vision, holding a shiny black pair of binoculars. I swiftly grabbed them and swung them toward the mysterious boater just in time to see the man at the stern again, bending over the bucket once more.

"I still can't see anything, and I don't understand," I said, lowering the binoculars. "What's he doing? What *could* he be doing?"

The heavyset man knelt by the bucket, oblivious to the two police cruisers, the coroner's car, and the dozen crime scene onlookers on the beach.

"Are you going to talk to the police?" Ayla

asked. "I mean, it's pretty obvious that this guy's up to no good."

"I don't know if we can trust the police." I glanced at Ayla.

"Okay. Who can we trust?"

"I don't know."

"Oh," Ayla said, her tone falling. "I thought you had an idea."

I looked at my youngest sister and chuckled. "If anything in a case comes together that quickly, Ayla, it's likely not to be trusted. Or you live a charmed life."

She looked at me oddly. "We do live a charmed life. We're witches."

"Tell that to Amelia."

I turned back toward the boat, but the man was gone.

* * *

"COME ON! WE'RE GOING BOATING."

My three sisters and dozens upon dozens of fish stared at me like I'd just announced we would burn the place down to roast marshmallows.

"Are you feeling okay?" Althea asked.

"I'm feeling great! We're on vacation, we decided we'd go boating today, and Amelia arranged for us to take out that great big luxurious yacht thing at the dock. We should take advantage of it. Get some sea air." As I spoke, I'd casually worked my way over to the key that closed the panels and moved to hide the fishtanks behind the walls. "Come on, no one has to go fishing, but I think we need to get out of this condo for a bit. Get some fresh air."

I turned the key, and the wall panels whirred to life.

Ami smirked as the fish swam frantically into the still-exposed parts of the tank, griping and complaining as the ever-smaller space became more and more crowded. They seemed so intent, so determined. And yet they were trapped there, unable to stop the wall from closing no matter how hard they begged.

"Okay, what are you—" Ami asked, but my finger held up to my lips cut her question off.

"I'm going to go change. Is there a specific type of clothing we should wear?" I joked. I heard the wall panel slam into place behind me as I walked down the hall to the main bedroom. I needed to get some things from my duffel bag.

"Astra change? Okay, now I know she's up to something," Althea said.

Charles seemed confused as I asked him for the keys to the yacht on the dock, reminding him that Amelia had arranged for us to take the boat out. Despite his surprise, he didn't argue and handed the keys over with a polite nod. "It's getting late," he told me. "Since you don't know the area, you may want to make sure you're back before sunset. All the docks tend to look the same at night."

"I'll be fine," I told him. "I'm a good navigator, but I'll keep it in mind."

"Okay," he said, then he pushed his hands into his pockets and looked away. "Well, have fun. Maybe we'll see you later."

Charles did not sound like he wanted us to have fun, but he didn't seem to know what else to say.

"Come on, guys, let's get this boat out to sea," I said. Ami, Althea, and Ayla followed me to the dock (still confused about why we were going at all), and we walked the short distance to the luxurious yacht Amelia had reserved for us.

I was familiar enough with boats in general to see the way this small yacht was lovingly maintained, but regardless I walked the length of the boat, checking the vessel's safety and stability. Then I climbed aboard.

It had wicker chairs, a bar, and a decorative captain's wheel on a deck the size of two Hummers. Well-appointed, yes—but decorated in colors that wouldn't look out of place in a Las Vegas funhouse.

It wasn't the largest, most lavish motor yacht I'd ever been on, but it *was* a yacht. A cabin cruiser set up for leisurely entertaining.

I took a brief break from my inspection of the cruiser to look down into the small boat tied up next to the yacht on the dock, but it was empty, and there was no sign of a bucket on its scuffed deck.

Darn it.

Once I was certain that everything was in order (and there were no paranormal beings or secret assassins hiding within), I went out onto the deck and called to my sisters to join me. "Okay, come on. Though, technically, you're supposed to ask me for permission to come aboard."

Ami raised an eyebrow, and Althea's eyes flitted between the two of us once they'd made their way on board. "What are we even doing out here?"

"Are you okay?" Althea asked as she stepped beside me.

I tilted my head. "Do you want to talk without hundreds of fish listening?"

Ayla frowned. "I don't mean to be unsupportive of the plan you clearly have that you're not bothering to share with us, but I just think maybe it doesn't make sense to go all the way to the ocean for that."

Althea nodded. "That does seem rather impractical."

I nodded and then, with a flourish, slipped the silver key into the black slot on the control panel, turned it, and listened to the powerful engine rumble to life. I then eased the throttle forward and allowed the *Delora Naudia* to drift away from the dock.

"Sit down," I called over my shoulder. "And put on your life jackets."

"Life jackets? What do we need those for?"

"I'll show you if you put them on."

Twenty seconds later, all three sisters called back to let me know they had their jackets on and were sitting down. Luckily, my military uniform had a wide variety of defensive and supportive water spells woven in, and I didn't need one.

Gently, I pushed forward on the "stern control" and brought the boat into deeper water.

Then I grasped the throttle and pushed it forward.

Hard.

The engine roared into action, propelling the boat forward. It took off away from the dock and glided across the calm waters of the ocean, much like a fish swimming against the flow of the current. Ahead of us, the sun was setting, painting the sky in shades of orange and red.

I took the wheel and pushed the throttle forward. The waves lapped against the bow, and I felt a sense of exhilaration despite all that was happening.

I wanted to get away from Amelia's building, away from the undines I didn't trust, away from the shore where my cousin's body lay lifeless in the sand.

But more important, I wanted to get out into the ocean, an ocean that all these people seemed to struggle over.

* * *

I THROTTLED the boat engine down when we were a mile away from shore. I could make out the silhouettes of buildings in Cocoa Beach, but they were lost and indistinguishable from the rest of the world behind us.

The water was calmer here, and we drifted.

"Everyone okay?" I asked, joining my sisters on the deck.

"You drive like a crazy person," Althea told me. It was more of a statement than a judgment, really. "I don't think you're supposed to go that fast in the no-wake zone, you know. And I think you swamped the seagulls."

Althea did have a point. From what I could see, there were a lot of seagulls gathering in the distance, probably trying to regroup. But it was hard to tell.

"Okay, now can you tell us what's going on?" Ayla asked, gripping one of the wicker arms of the deck chair. "Why did you bring us out here?"

"We're out of earshot now," I said. "No fish people to listen in."

She gave me an arch look. "You mean the undines."

"Look, one thing I can tell you from working cases is that we—Emma and I—often need to talk through possibilities. Right now, we're staying in a place where the walls have ears. Literally." I looked around at my sisters. "We're in the middle of someone else's drama. We don't know any of the players. We don't know what's going on, not really. We don't even know much about the town. And we're trying to figure it out while under aquatic surveillance."

"So you brought us out here to...?" Althea's question ended openly.

"So we could talk freely. Talk through what we know, and plan our next move." I sat back in my chair. "And since we're being listened to all the time, anyway, we might be able to use that somehow."

"Disinformation, you mean?"

I nodded.

Ami looked unsure. "You're sure they can't hear us out here?"

"We're a mile away, the wind is blowing, and the engine is off. The fish in that building can't hear us. That's for sure. But as you pointed out," I said, glancing at Ayla, "this is the ocean. I don't know what's beneath the surface."

"I don't know." Ayla leaned forward, desperate. "What if we're being tracked?"

I took a deep breath of salty air and looked up at Archie hovering above us, beating his mammoth wings to create an updraft to keep him aloft. He circled the boat once, spotted us, and swooped toward the deck. As he neared, he shouted, "She's coming! Look alive! She's headed right toward you!"

"Who is?" I called up. "What—"

The silver mermaid leaped onto the deck with a dull thud, hurtling out of the water. Her tail was a blur of movement, and she twisted in midair, turning her snow-white fin into a battering ram. She smashed Ayla's wicker deck chair into splinters, and my youngest sister flew off the starboard side of the yacht into the dark waters below.

CHAPTER EIGHT

*T*he mermaid tilted her head and rolled her eyes, slowly lowering her gaze to the splintered remains of the chair.

My body tensed as her opalescent fins brushed against the wood grain. I knew Ayla was wearing a life jacket and that the boat, which was drifting freely, wasn't churning water with its deadly propellers. So she was probably fine.

Well.

There was a better than even chance she was okay.

"I can get Ayla," Ami murmured as she fixed her gaze on the fish woman. The mermaid's hair was long and silky, falling behind her like a white cape, and her stormy blue eyes fixed on my sister.

"There's a lifebuoy over there. Can you handle this?"

Obviously.

I was on alert.

I was poised and ready to attack, ready to defend us if necessary. I'd never fought a mermaid before, but it didn't matter. I'd fought almost every other type of creature, so I wasn't worried about facing fillet of attitude over there.

"I'm fine. Get Ayla."

"Yes, locate the death speaker and extricate her from the water before it ends up killing her," the mermaid says, her face still and expressionless. "Today, my people are particularly defensive and the ocean is no place for land crawlers."

"Land crawlers. Right. Um, all right. I'll be back," Ami said, glancing over her shoulder before she stepped toward the side and walked away.

As Ami ran for the orange high-visibility safety donut, the mermaid's eyes followed her toward the rail—almost as if she considered stopping her. Moving nothing but her intense blue eyes, she fixed her gaze on me. "If you're going to express gratitude to me for allowing your companion to survive, do so quickly. I have additional inquiries."

Express gratitude?

For the fish woman's aerial attack on my boat? Not likely.

"I'm not grateful," I told her flatly. "I'm annoyed. You've jumped on my boat and knocked my sister into the ocean."

"Your boat is not your boat," she said. The mermaid's eyes were flat, uninterested—like she was bored listening to me. She played with the seaweed in her long hair, rolling the strands between three fingers. "However, I suppose that is irrelevant to someone who is content to be borrowed by the humans."

"Excuse me?" The boat bobbed like a buoy in the water as the two of us spoke, the sky growing dark as the sun set. "Borrowed by humans? What does that mean?"

"You are disturbed because of the state of your body, the constant transition and movement. You are unaware of how to control or handle your current mass and energy, but you will," she explained, her voice low and melodic and, seemingly, right at my ears despite the distance between us. Her tail flapped on the deck with thuds of impatience. "However, that is not the primary concern at the moment."

"Who's primary concern? I have no idea what you're talking about," I said, glancing over my shoulder at the ruined chair and back to the fish woman.

"Naturally."

As annoyed as I was, I had to admit the mermaid was stunningly beautiful. She shimmered ever so slightly and her scales reminded me of pearls. But it was her eyes, her bright blue eyes, that held me. "Who are you? How about we start there?"

She gave me a look of disgust. "Previously, your kind would summon me for assistance with all things water-related, but you have no idea who I am now." Her cold eyes narrowed. "Your cousin knew me well."

"And now she's dead," I responded with a hard glare. "So you see my concern here."

"Yes," she said. "You are concerned that you will lose your sisters and you will be alone."

I blinked. "My concern is that you won't tell me everything I need to know." I tilted my head. "I don't know who you are, but I'm pretty sure you're going to tell me within the next few seconds, or I'm going to fillet you like a—"

"Okay, okay, let's calm down," Archie cockily interrupted from his perch on the railing of his boat. The immense owl flapped at me, regarding me with dark eyes. Long claws clutched the bar. "No one's attacked anyone just yet—"

"Yeah, I beg to differ here," Ayla said as she and Ami returned to the hot deck. Ayla's clothes were dripping wet and clung to her like a second skin. She smelled like wet seaweed. "Maybe that was accidental, but it sure felt like an attack."

The mermaid didn't laugh or smile as Althea wrapped Ayla in a blanket. Wet and shivering, she stood against the railing with Ami leaning against her, hugging her.

"Who are you?" I asked again, trying to keep my voice steady.

"I am Eisheth," she announced with a nod.

Althea gasped. "Hold up, hold up. From the Kabbalah? The princess of the Qliphoth?"

"What's a Qliphoth?" I asked.

"Evil or impure spiritual forces in Jewish mysticism."

"So, paranormals," Ayla said with an eye roll.

"Well, maybe," Althea said, thinking. "In mystical theory, the Judeo-Christian god created them to prevent the flow of divinity (revelation of God's true unity) from dissipating as it pervades the various facets of Creation. They conceal holiness, kind of. Act as shells to protect it. Well, originally." She shrugged. "Eventually, man decided they were demons that needed to be destroyed."

"Color me shocked," Ami murmured. Althea looked at her. "What? I'm just not surprised that's what happened, are you?"

"Are you that Eisheth?" I asked her. "The one from her book?"

Althea made a face. "Well, it's not my book, it's—"

"I don't care," I told her, cutting her off. "Come on, fish woman. Are you that Eisheth?"

Eisheth narrowed her eyes. "I am. I am Eisheth and where I was, I am still."

I blinked. "So you're a...?"

"Angel," Ami said, slowly. "She's an actual *angel*."

"No way," I said, shaking my head.

"I was a guardian angel on earth. Once," the mermaid said with a shrug. "I've transformed into a guardian angel in the water."

"Lateral transfer?" I asked. "Do angels have bureaucracy?"

"Astra!" Ami hissed.

"We protect those who seek our assistance,"

she continued, ignoring my barbs. "The ocean requires assistance, which is why I am here. You small land creatures appear to spend your entire existence attempting to kill and maim everything in your path. You pollute and destroy your world. You are a scourge." Her scowl could be heard in her voice. "You are very annoying creatures, but as my origin is angelic, I cannot kill you despite all your considerable stupidity." She sniffed. "Much as I would like to."

"Okay, at least you're a little less vague," I murmured, glancing at my sisters. "Now that we know who you claim to be, why are you here? Why did you jump on our boat?"

"Because this is the last place I saw Amelia, and no one but Amelia uses this boat." Her blue eyes flashed with anger. "If you killed her, I will kill you all for your crime."

* * *

THE OCEAN BREEZE rippled through the silvery-white hair of the mermaid Eisheth, who sat on the edge of the boat and stared out into the darkening water. She sighed as she tapped her fingertips on the side of the boat, then glanced back at the five of us as we talked.

"Do we believe her?" Ami asked.

The boat bobbed up and down and up and down.

"There *are* things like the things Althea pulled from her encyclopedic brain," Archie admitted. He turned his head this way and that, causing his tufts of white feathers to sway in the darkness. "If she is who she says she is, she likely has dominion over this section of ocean."

"Dominion?" I leaned on the railing of the boat and stared out at the water. The ocean was dark and blue and endless, with little white waves dancing like wild dogs on the sand. "That's a strong word. Is she evil? Or angelic? Who's book is right? Again, we've met someone mysterious from Amelia's life, and again, she might have been a partner—or might have been the person that killed her."

"I don't know about you guys, but she doesn't look like an angel to me," Ayla said. "Angel, demon, whatever..." She paused. "I don't see wings, so I'm guessing not an angel."

"It's not that simple," Althea told Ayla. "Angel is a misnomer, almost," Althea admitted. "They are actually spiritual creatures that are revealed within the Tree of Life. They also belong to the—"

"You know, does it really matter?" I asked, turning back from the railing to stare at my sisters. "Does what she was five thousand years ago really matter? Does a passage in an old book —that's probably been reworked hundreds of times over thousands of years to bend its beliefs to the ones men wanted represented—matter? Angel, demon, mermaid, Little Mermaid—we're not taking a paranormal census here." The waves rocked the boat, sending drops of saltwater splashing against my face. "Don't get distracted by the big picture. We have two questions to answer right now before any other questions can be asked."

"And they are?" Althea asked with a shrug as she leaned back on the edge of the boat.

"Can we trust her, and are we in danger from her?"

"Only I can answer that question," Eisheth called from the stern of the ship, gliding her delicate hand over the hull as if petting a great leviathan.

The five of us turned to stare at her.

She brought her hands to her face and tapped the tip of her index finger against her full pink lips before fluttering them open. "Unless, of course, you are willing to take my hand, Astra Arden of the Coven Athenian."

She held out her hand toward me.

"I'm not going to do that," I told her.

Eisheth shrugged. "So be it," she said, dropping her hand. "I was unaware of your cowardice. That was unexpected." Eisheth flicked her silver hair off her shoulder and leaned back.

"Hello, no, I'm not!" I snapped, standing straight and glaring at her. "But Amelia did drown in the ocean, and from where I sit, you look perfectly positioned to drown someone. Mermaid, right? So you have hydrokinesis powers?"

"Water manipulation?" Ayla asked.

Althea nodded.

"You know what our bodies contain more than anything else?" I asked Ayla.

"Water."

"That's right. Up to 60 percent. Hydrokinesis is nothing to play around with."

The mermaid's skin illuminated faintly as if moonlight was emanating from her. Her eyes caught each of us, as if she could see our every thought. "If I wanted you dead," she said, "this boat would already be on the ocean floor." Her eyes locked with mine. "If you will not use the goddess within you, the powers the universe gave you, why bother to have them, star woman? Are they wasted on you?" The wind ruffled her long white hair, sending it swirling over her shoulders. "I know you now. It is only your fear that stops you from knowing me."

"Oh, for gods' sake. It's like dealing with a Sphinx," I muttered. "And I'd like to point out I never trusted them, either."

"Trust? Only I can answer that," Eisheth said from the stern, tipping her head to the side and looking at me like a cat would look at a bird. "Only you can determine if what I say is truth."

I felt a surge of power within me. The power that had burned in me since the day I was reborn, that rushed through me when I uncaged the stupid owl who had appeared on my doorstep. I knew it was there, but I'd never used it much, and (to be totally honest) I had no idea how it could help me now.

"What do you think?" I asked, looking at Archie.

The boat rocked.

"What if it's a trick?" Ami asked, leaning forward, squinting at the mermaid. "What if she's a siren?"

I stopped. "A siren?" I repeated, my mouth

hanging open. "Can we not make this situation even more complicated?" Ami held her hands up and shrugged. "Aren't they half-bird half-woman?"

"Granted, she's not singing, but Astra—everything Eisheth says could be a lie. And if she is a siren, *you* have to go to *her* before she can drown you. Once you do that, though, her power explodes in full force."

"Sirens are far from mermaids, though," Althea told Ami.

"Sirens lie," Ami retorted. "And both are shapeshifters. The song is likely just myth, but the choice to follow giving them power? That's no myth."

"I am the guardian." Eisheth's voice was strong, sure. "I am the guardian of the sea, and I have not lied. I have not misled."

"Or everything you say is a lie. One of the two," I muttered.

"Okay, let's just say you're right, Ami. So, if you're right, just so everyone's clear, the call works in three phases," Althea started. "The first is the allure, which can be broken if the victim maintains their belief that the siren can't be trusted. The second is the hypnosis, which is where the victim believes that any action the siren performs is actually of their own free will even though it's not."

"Uh-huh," I said, nodding. "And phase three is?"

"The drowning."

* * *

THE STANDOFF on the deck continued.

"This is absurd. If I had intended to murder you, you would have drowned long ago," Eisheth repeated again. "How do you land crawlers get anything done? Time races past you like steam from an engine."

Eisheth turned her head to the other side, fluttering her silvery-white hair off her shoulder and back down to her chest. "I am not a siren, nor are sirens and mermaids the same." She paused, then turned her gaze to my sisters. "None of you have any reason to trust me, but even in your fear you should at least be wise enough witches to feel instinctively that I am not a threat to your lives." She raised an eyebrow. "At least not at this moment."

I tilted my head back and closed my eyes.

From the moment I decided to take out the yacht, I'd felt a strong, almost irresistible urge to head out into the ocean. That sudden urge to head out into the middle of the ocean worried me. It was making me fear grabbing the mermaid's hand.

Eisheth clearly knew us.

Well, knew me.

No, us. She'd called Ayla a death speaker.

And that added to my concern.

The boat rocked.

Amelia, a Hex Master, drowned. Her body washed up on the beach. This wasn't cowardice, I told myself. I had every reason not to trust an ancient being mentioned in the freaking Kabbalah. One that lived beneath the surface of the world I lived in, and who resented those that made their home on the land.

Granted, I sighed, that one was pretty well-earned. Humankind abused the ocean like it was their own personal kiddie pool.

I opened my eyes and looked at the mermaid. I took a step toward Eisheth, then paused again. My mind filled with questions, but I doubted she'd be willing to give me answers—and I doubted I would believe her answers, anyway.

Not until I took her hand.

And I still didn't know if I should.

"What does she want?" I asked myself out

loud, returning to my position on the edge of the boat. "And did she bring us here?"

"All good questions," Archie told me uselessly, bobbing his fluffy head.

"I was not the one who brought you here." Eiseth's bright blue eyes, flecked with green, narrowed at me as the ocean breeze whipped her snow-colored hair into a frenzy. Her face had softened since we began talking and I could see the scars on her skin from battles beneath the water. Her furrowed brow relaxed and she sighed. "Arden women, I sensed you here. I suspected you were on your way to me. You, Astra, were the one who called to me. And I think you know that."

"I did?" I asked. "Okay, say I did. Why?"

"It is your magic that brought you and your sisters here." She shook her head. "Or perhaps it is more accurate to say it is your need."

"What do you mean?"

"You know," she said, stopping. "You *know*." Eiseth reached out a hand.

"No, you don't," I said, putting my hands behind my back. "I'm asking because I don't know. Answer me first."

The mermaid tilted her head to the side and let her hair fall back around her shoulder. Her eyes closed and she sighed. "Trust your abilities, witch, or else we're all going to spend the night on this boat. A storm is approaching, and I'd rather be beneath the waves when it hits." Eisheth's eyes opened, the moonlight reflecting off them. "For me to trust you, you must trust me. There is no other way."

Ayla grunted. "Ugh. All we need is answers. You're making this a leap of faith for Astra, you know. That's not fair."

"That is your need, the answers," Eisheth agreed. "You, who are seen in the darkness and who walk in the light, you are always reaching out to a greater power. Why are you surprised that Astra must learn to do the same to move forward?"

"You seem to know more and more things about me the longer you're on this boat," I said.

"I know many things about you." Eisheth tilted her head, sending her hair cascading down her back. "More than we have time for right now." Her eyes narrowed. "I sense there is so much more to discuss, but I cannot have this conversation any longer." She looked at me. "You must make your choice."

The moon shone down on the boat, casting a silvery light on the dark waters. The boat rocked gently, the waves no longer choppy. The weather had been warm when we went out, but now it was cool.

"How long do I have?" I asked.

"Not long," she told me. "The storm will come, and I will go."

I stared at her for a second.

The boat rocked again.

I took a step toward the mermaid and pulled my gloves from my hands.

CHAPTER NINE

The water was cold and dark. I could see sunlight drifting down in rays on the shallow sand she hovered over. Amelia. It's Amelia. Underneath, in the deep, murky water, I saw Amelia.

I could see the fear in her eyes.

As I tried to swim to her, I felt a tight panic in my chest, but it was futile. I thrashed around in confusion as a school of fish blocked my path, pushing me further and further away. Lights flashed in my eyes, and the water was thick with bubbles, making it difficult to see. I moved and moved some more, but I couldn't get to her. "Oh, man," I murmured, trying to release Eisheth's hands. "I think I'm going to be sick."

"Watch," Eisheth whispered, and I felt her squeeze my hands tighter.

The water churned and threw me forward. The images in my mind were as clear as if I were there, and I could feel myself roar with rage and frustration beneath the waterline. Amelia was alone and vulnerable, just out of reach, and someone was attempting to harm her. I knew I had to help her, but the fish encircled us, snarling as if to mock me. Colors and bubbles spun all around, and I couldn't focus on anything beyond her terrified face beneath the water getting smaller and smaller, and her—

I yanked my hands away from the mermaid's, turned, and threw myself over the railing, just in time to vomit the contents of my stomach into the sea. I'd never felt so ill in my entire life. Every breath was agony against the bitter bile that kept rising up, bile that tasted like the sea.

"Astra?"

I was vaguely aware of someone coming up to me, but I couldn't focus on anything. All I could do was retch in the most unladylike of ways until there was nothing left in me.

"Astra?" the voice whispered again more urgently.

I shook my head and raised my hand to tell

whoever it was to leave me alone. The nausea was unlike anything I'd ever felt before, and vertigo in my head made the boat feel as if it were being tossed and turned in a typhoon. I just wanted to lean against this surface and die with the strong taste of bitter saltwater in my mouth, so the world would stop spinning.

I felt a touch on my shoulder, and I flinched for reasons I didn't understand. It was nothing to be afraid of, though. The contact was gentle, and so was the voice. "Astra, can you hear me?"

It was just Ami.

I nodded.

With one last retching heave, I slumped over the railing, weak and spent.

"I think I'm dying," I groaned.

Ami leaned down to inspect me, and I saw a flash of amusement. Her gaze was drawn to mine, and I could see the concern and worry on her face. "You're not dying. You're just out of it— which is not entirely unexpected. You just looked through the eyes of a mermaid." She smoothed the hair from my sweaty brow. "Considering what that did to you, I hope you got some information out of it."

I tried to smile, but I didn't have the energy

for it. "I saw something. I'm just…not sure what it was that I saw."

She reached over to wrap her arm around my waist, allowing me to lean on her for support. "Maybe we should ask Eisheth, then. If you think we can trust her. Though even if we can't, you probably need to ask her."

I shook my head. "I think so. Well, mostly. She cared about Amelia somehow. I do know she didn't want her to die. I don't know that translates into her being trustworthy, but she probably has the same goals. Find Amelia's killer."

Ami shook her head, her long hair spilling over her face as she leaned even closer. "Astra, you look so pale. I think you should sit down." She half-dragged me to the deck chair, and I collapsed on it. "What in the world did that mermaid show you? Can you tell us?" Ami asked.

I nodded, trying to collect myself. "I saw Amelia beneath the ocean, but she had no scuba gear on, no breathing apparatus. It could have been a spell, but—" I glanced about the boat, trying to gather my thoughts. Eisheth watched me intently. "Wait a minute. Amelia looked like a mermaid. She had fins just like that." I pointed weakly.

My sisters—and Archie—looked shocked by

my words. All four mouths—well, three mouths and one beak—fell open as they stared from me to the mermaid.

Disbelief shot across his face as the words, "How is that possible?" echoed across the deck. His tone was belligerent.

"Weren't you sent here by a god to help us with questions like that?" Ayla asked dryly. "I thought you knew almost everything there was to know?"

"You know, I was reading about Athena's owl the other day. The historical references, not Archie specifically," Althea told Ayla. "Hegel—the philosopher—had this fascinating quote about the divine owl as a metaphor. He thought the owl represented understanding in the 'maturity of reality.' You know, like, hindsight? Because the owl only spreads its wings at dusk."

"I can spread my wings any time I want!" Archie snapped, his feathers ruffling with annoyance. "I hunt at night because I can see better than everyone! And no one can see me coming!" He gave a loud hoot. "Philosophers. What idiots."

"Well, do you have any other observations?" Ayla asked him. "Any information that could shed some light on what Astra saw?"

"Do I? Do *I?*" The owl paced back and forth on the railing, his feathers ruffled. He gave another loud hoot and looked around with a sour expression. Finally, he turned an icy gaze on Ayla. "Well. No."

"Don't be snide, then," Ayla told him.

I wanted to defend Archie...but I was exhausted.

All I wanted was to sleep, to let the certainty of dreams take me away from the confusing images in my mind. The images I saw through the frustrated eyes of Eisheth, the angelic Cocoa Beach mermaid. I looked at her wearily—she sat regally along the railing, her expression still cold. "You saw her drown," I said almost absently.

"I saw her drown," Eisheth said with a nod.

"You tried to save her."

The mermaid nodded once, a flash of pain cracking through her stern exterior.

"I don't understand," Althea said, her expression confused. "You're a mermaid, and this is the ocean. I mean, I assume she drowned in the ocean, right?" My sister looked at me, and I nodded. She turned to look at Eisheth, and her eyes narrowed. "What good's an angelic guardian with dominion over the ocean if a lifebuoy works better? Why couldn't you save her?"

"It's not her fault. She tried. The fish wouldn't let her," I said.

My bookish sister's eyes went wide with shock. "The fish? Fish drowned Amelia?"

"Not fish," Eisheth responded. "Undines."

Lightning flashed.

* * *

THE CLOUDS WERE black and heavy, and the wind was picking up. We all stood up—well, everyone but the mermaid—on the deck, turning to watch the storm. The waves were getting bigger and bigger, and the wind was howling. As if on cue, a wave hit the side of the boat, rocking it back and forth.

"I must go," Eisheth said, and she turned her body toward the choppy water. "If you need me once the storm passes, call, and I will come."

I shook my head. "Wait, I have more questions."

"No."

And with that, the odd mermaid dove into the water and was gone.

"Did we really just spend hours out here to find out she saw Amelia drown and that undines may have done it?" Althea fumed, a fierce look on her face. "She could have told us that two seconds after her angelic fish butt hit the deck. So what was the purpose of that whole song and dance?"

"Mermaids are weird," Ayla said with a shrug.

Althea opened her mouth to respond, but no words came out. She shut her mouth again, looking irritated.

"I understand everyone is frustrated. I don't know about you," Ami, the quiet peacekeeper, began, her voice soft and gentle, "but I think we should get back to shore. Astra, can you drive? None of the rest of us know how."

"Yeah, I can, and you're right," I agreed. "That storm looks nasty."

"I think that's the most sensible thing you've said all day." Althea turned and walked toward the door leading down to the cabin. "We still need to find a place to talk. The sooner we figure that out, the better."

I steered the boat back toward the condo at a brisk but controlled pace. It bobbed against the waves, but I held it steady. As we crossed the inlet, I could see the storm moving in from the Atlantic side, lightning teasing overhead. The thunder growled, and the rain grew heavier.

"A shame we couldn't have talked to the

mermaid more," Ami said as she leaned back in her deck chair and closed her eyes.

"I feel like all powerful paranormal creatures like to play games. It's annoying," Althea said from the back of the boat. "I expect if we need her, though, we'll be able to find her. She spent a lot of time with us for some reason."

As I headed toward the dock, I realized that it wasn't just her eyes I'd seen through. Her whole ball of emotional turmoil, her authentic self—I'd felt it all. I'd felt the fear like I was there and going through it. Tasted the sea. I shook with frustration and anger, felt the fury in my own gut. It wasn't often my psychometry picked up on so many aspects of a situation, and certainly not all at once.

"Water," Ami murmured, patting my shoulder.

"What?"

"Water provides natural properties to enhance and strengthen psychic communication," she explained. "It intensifies metaphysical abilities. Water is capable of supporting life. It has carved continents out of the land. It can either cause devastation or provide comfort. Water is a fantastic conductor. That's why your experience was far beyond what you've experienced before."

Archie jumped onto the helm station. "Yeah, what she said."

"Yeah, what she said?" I mocked. "You really haven't been much help, you know."

"I'm a bird, you ninny!" he huffed, defensive.

"Here," Althea said, holding out something to me. "Drink this. It will help. I found some stuff in the galley below. That should settle your stomach, at least."

"Oh, thanks," I said. I gulped it down and welcomed the bitter taste—then turned back to Archie. "What do you mean, you're a bird? What does that have to do with anything?"

"I'm of the air, not the water. If you see an owl swimming, we're swimming for our lives. Last resort. Got ourselves in a pickle. I can do it, but believe you me, I would never choose to," he told me forcefully. "We have no means of defense in the water. None. Zip. Zilch. Zero. And when we get out, we can't fly until we dry." He blinked. "I hate the water."

"You hate everything," Ayla said dismissively.

Archie looked so angry I thought he was about to explode. "I am of the *air*. The air. Not the water. The water? That's the *only* thing that scares me."

"Oh," Ayla said, sounding mildly mollified. "Good to know."

I carefully maneuvered through the roiling sea, following rusty buoys toward the dock. The waves rocked the small vessel violently, and I had to fight to keep my cool and keep the boat steady. Finally, we bumped against the dock with a hard clang. "I'm sorry," I told him as we tied up the boat. "I didn't know."

"Yeah, you people never notice anything. I am a bird of *prey*. I am not a cuddly little parakeet that you can put on your shoulder and take everywhere. I have claws, I have a beak, and I have talons. I am not a pet. I am a natural predator," Archie continued. "But I belong in the *sky*, not the *water*."

"Archie, we didn't mean—"

"You did. You did." The owl was definitely not impressed with our attempt at understanding or my apology. "I flew all over the ocean today following the stupid mermaid. It was a long day. My wings got tired. I was hungry, and you know how I get when I'm hungry." Archie's dark eyes widened with incredulity. "All you could do was criticize me for not knowing about an element that has nothing to do with me. Nothing."

Wow, Archie was mad. "I'm sorry," I repeated.

"Whatever," Archie said, turning his back and spreading his wings. And with that, he fluffed his feathers, ruffled his wings, and then leaped into the air.

"That went well," Althea said.

"Not sure what happened because I didn't catch all of it," a voice called from the dock, "but maybe things will start looking up now that we're here."

* * *

"THERE ARE certain benefits to having the captain date his mother," Detective Emma Sullivan, my best friend, said as she hitched her thumb toward Jason Bishop, my boyfriend. The salt air blew her hair around her face, but she didn't even notice. "Some ghost friends of your cousin told his mother what was going on down here. She called him. He called me—and a quick follow-up call to your mother made it clear you hadn't told her squat."

"Hi," Jason said, raising his hand. "I tried to call you. I really did," he explained with an embarrassed look on his face. "But your phone just kept going to voice mail. We tried your sisters, too." He leaned to the side and waved at them. "We decided to head down after we couldn't get a hold of any of you." He glanced at the yacht. "Nice boat."

In the bay, the storm churned, and the waves grew higher. "Thanks," I said as a gust of wind blew my hair across my face. "Look, let's get inside." I gestured toward the building before scrambling off the yacht.

"Hold up. You really think we should explain all this in there?" Althea asked. "Considering the mermaid just accused the undines of participating in Amelia's murder, that might be the last place we want to go."

"Mermaid?" Jason asked, his confused face revealing his innocence.

"What's an undine?" Emma added, her eyes wide with excited curiosity.

"Someone who might be involved in Amelia's murder," I said. "And yes, there's a mermaid in the ocean."

"You do know what a mermaid is, right?" Ayla asked.

"Of course. I watch Disney movies. It's a mythical creature that's half human, half fish," Emma explained. "Sings show tunes, collects forks."

"Yep. That is a mermaid," I told her. "Except for that last part."

"Mermaids aren't real, though," Emma said firmly.

"Says the woman with the vampire brother and the witch best friend," Ayla laughed disdainfully. "Always amazes me you humans have to deny something's existence as a go to. Why don't you try asking questions first? Learning?"

Althea glared at her. "I thought we dropped the attitude?"

Ayla shrugged.

"Ayla, that's not nice," Ami said, looking a little more than uncomfortable.

"We don't have to go to the condo," Jason said (as if trying to change the subject before all the women started in on each other). "I got a room for us at the Babylon Hotel. We didn't know how fast we'd be able to find you, so I thought it best to get us a place to stay just in case."

"You two got a room at the Babylon Hotel?" Ayla asked, her expression dubious. "The one that blares 'I'm too sexy' over and over on the loudspeaker and looks a little like a French brothel?"

"Yes. We did," Jason replied, his arms crossed

over his chest. "It's just across the street from the condo. Why?"

"Ayla," Ami said, her voice a warning.

"No reason," Ayla said quickly.

"I'm sure it's nice." I shrugged.

"I'm sure it's *not*," Althea said. "It's a sexy spring break hotel. Unfortunately, it probably sounds—and smells—like a bacchanal."

Ayla rolled her eyes. "And you would know how that sounds and smells how?"

Althea sniffed. "I'm insulted by that question. We all know I'm the erudite sister."

"What's erudite mean?" Ayla asked.

"If you were the erudite sister, you'd know."

"Before it starts raining, I'd like to remind you all I have a place to go," Jason smiled. "Apart from its hints of bacchanalia, it was close, and I got a suite, so there's plenty of room."

"I was in it. I'm sure it'll be fine," Emma said, running her hand through her hair. The wind picked up, and she shivered. "It's freezing out here. Wherever we're going to go, can we just go? I want to get some hot coffee and hear about the situation down here."

"Right." I glanced at the weather.

This morning, it had been in the eighties. By the time night rolled around, the temperature had dropped, and I saw no evidence that the storm was anywhere near over. For all I knew, it would get worse.

I turned back to the others. "The Babylon Hotel," I told them firmly. "It's probably better we talk this through without anyone overhearing us."

"Sounds like a plan," Jason said, gesturing toward the street. "Lead the way."

"As always," Ayla muttered under her breath as we walked down the dock.

CHAPTER TEN

"*I*t's like the inside of Hugh Hefner's brain," Althea laughed, tossing her jacket on a chair. The woven rug and magenta silk couch clashed violently, creating a cacophony of color. She approached the bar and peered inside at the expensive bottles, shaking her head. "I don't think I've ever seen a tackier hotel room."

"I have," I told her, shuddering. "But not by much."

The beds were the color of strawberry ice cream, with pink silk sheets and pillows. A small kitchenette with a refrigerator, microwave, and coffee maker sat between the door and one of the beds. A sliding glass door led out to a balcony with a view of the ocean.

"Yeah, I know." Emma looked around. "Tacky. I hear you."

The room smelled like stale cigarette smoke and spilled beer—and gods only know what else. However, that foundational smell was covered by perfumed scents of vanilla and flowers as if dozens of scented candles had been lit all at once to cover the aroma of old, tired room.

"Again, I chose it for the location," Jason explained, looking slightly embarrassed. "My taste in hotels tends to more understated accommodations."

Though it was technically a suite (and a relatively large one), it felt small and cramped. The ceilings were low, and the furniture was cheap, gaudy, and plentiful. There was a large flat-screen television on the wall in front of a sitting area, along with a small coffee table. A small door to my left was partially open, revealing a bathtub and sink. The inside of the bathroom had been painted with an eggshell frost, and though it didn't look fancy, it seemed like it would be relaxing.

Not my style, but I was just relieved to be in a warm room—and the thing I cared about most was the coffee maker.

Well, Jason.

And Emma and my sisters.

Then the coffee maker.

"Isn't that nice?" Ayla smiled as she sat on the wine-colored couch and curled her feet up underneath her. "I mean, it's ugly as sin—and, come to think of it, this couch has probably seen more than one sin in its day—but it's comfortable. At least the ground's not rolling under my feet anymore."

"Let's admit it: this place is crazy," Emma said as she took a seat on the edge of the bed. "But, like Jason said—it was the closest to the condo."

Ami turned on the television and then turned down the volume completely.

"How did you two even wind up here?" I asked as I scooped coffee into the filter. The scent was earthy and spicy, with just a hint of sweetened cream. "In Cocoa Beach, I mean. You said your mother talked to a ghost that knew Amelia?"

Jason leaned back against the counter. "Mom called. She told me she got home from work and found a ghost in her living room."

"Really?" Jason's mother was the mayor of Cassandra, Florida—a place known for having the highest density of mediums in the entire world. Ghosts came and went from that psychic town like it was Grand Central Station for the dead. "Is that unusual somehow?"

"I don't think so," Jason replied. "What was unusual, though? She said it was a little kid and that the ghost was really upset about something—and even though it presented as a child, it was alone. That's not usual. Child ghosts tend to cluster together with other children or have an adult spirit with them."

"The mayor was pretty shaken when I talked to her," Emma agreed, frowning again. "The ghost was really young. Like, unusually young to be alone."

Jason nodded. "The ghost was so sad—and scared—that the kid wouldn't even talk to her for a bit. Finally, the girl told Mom that you were down here in trouble, that her friend had been murdered by her other friends, and that she didn't know what to do. When she called out for help, she wound up in Mom's house in the blink of an eye, and she wasn't quite sure how she got there." He looked at me. "Mom heard about your trip from the captain, and they were able to put two and two together. She tried calling you, but—"

"We were on the boat," I finished.

Jason nodded.

"The girl told the mayor Amelia was supposed to come with her, but she didn't get any more than that," Emma said, frowning. "She also said she saw something bad happen, and Amelia never came back out of the water again."

"She saw her friend, who was a selkie, go out to Amelia," Jason said. "And then they both were just gone."

"Saw a *selkie?*" I raised an eyebrow. Selkies were shapeshifters, and usually, their form was the seal. But a selkie could also become human, too. "You're sure she said selkie?"

He nodded.

I frowned.

Selkies rarely lived in Florida because there were no seal colonies in Florida. Harbor seals could be found, rarely, in inlets as far south as Volusia County, but we were well south of Volusia. Hooded seals rarely wandered this far south, if ever.

"She was crying and said something about her friend dying in the water," Jason said. "But then she just disappeared."

"She who? She the friend in the water, or she the ghost girl?"

"The ghost girl. Mom said she just vanished."

* * *

EVERYONE LOOKED EXHAUSTED. We'd spent a day on the boat in the sun, and as soon as we'd walked into the hotel, my sister's faces showed a smattering of sunburn.

"Let's take five minutes, get a drink, and unwind," I told the room. My sisters looked relieved before my suggestion was fully suggested. "I could use a few minutes to turn my brain off and enjoy the quiet."

"You'd think it would be quiet on a boat in the middle of the ocean," Ami agreed, walking toward the small kitchenette. "But trust me, there was something about being on the boat and at sea that made all of us talkative."

"Do you want anything, Jason?" I asked, frowning.

"For you to stop frowning," he said, reaching out to rub his fingers against my forehead. I noticed he did that often, gently reaching out to rub away any tension he saw on my face.

"Let me guess," he said, shaking his head. "You're thinking about what happened to Amelia."

I shrugged. "I can't stop thinking about it. Nothing about this situation makes sense, and it's so much more complicated than it should be. I usually have someone or something I can trust, but other than the people in this room, I don't trust anyone. And now a kid might be dead, too?" I picked up my coffee cup and took a long drink. "I don't like any of this. And I'm frustrated."

He smiled faintly. "I know."

"You know?" I looked at his handsome face, the gentle expression highlighted by eyes that shone with support and concern. "That's it? You've got to have something else to say," I said, surprised.

"I do not," he said firmly. "You've got to think. You've got to figure things out. And then you're going to do what you do, unapologetically."

"What if I don't figure things out?" I asked.

He reached out and pulled me toward him, lifting my chin so I was looking into his eyes. "You will," he promised. "I wish I could help you more. I don't have any powers like you and your sisters—or my mother. I don't even have a gun like Emma. All I can do is be here for you, support you, try and make sure you're okay." He smiled. "Though if there's some kind of trivial pursuit portion of this quest, I'll probably come in handy there."

"You're not trivial," I told him, smiling.

"I am, sometimes," he said. "But you're not." He leaned in and touched his lips to mine, kissing me softly. "You're tough, you're passionate, and you're smart. And those are the qualities that make you who you are. Those qualities won't let you down." He kissed me lightly again. "I know who you are, Astra."

I gave him a faint smile. "Well, that makes one of us."

"You're a powerful woman," he said, and his tone was steady and sure. "You're a good daughter, a good friend, a good psychic, and a good sister."

I looked at him. "But not a good detective?" I asked, frowning.

Jason blinked.

"Wow, that's your response to your boyfriend showering you with compliments and praise?" Althea asked. "You just dismiss all the sweet things he said and then hand him a bigger shovel so he can dig even deeper to prop up your ego?" She handed me a small tube. "Put that on your face. It'll keep that sunburn from getting worse."

"Thanks." I looked at Althea, took the tube, but before I could say anything else, she turned and headed out of the room.

"I know you're frustrated," Jason said, and

smiled. "And I know you're a good detective. It sounds like this situation is just really convoluted, Astra."

It was so nice to be back on solid ground, even if it was concrete. The hotel where Jason had secured the room wasn't anything fancy, but it was visibly clean (despite the embedded smells of occupants past) and quiet and had a great view of the ocean. As I walked back toward the window, I opened the curtains and looked out. The waves had become wild to the point of froth on top. "There's a whole world under there we don't know," I said to myself. "The mundane and the magical."

No one answered, or no one heard me.

I sighed and thought about the words Althea had said to me. Was it true that I dismissed all the compliments Jason gave me? Was I really so far in my head that I wouldn't accept a kind word when I heard it? I thought about it, then glanced over at Jason. "I'm sorry. I didn't mean to dismiss what you said like that," I said, softly. "Thanks for being here."

"You're welcome," he said, and smiled.

"I'm just frustrated," I said, "but I'm not powerless."

Jason raised an eyebrow. "Of course not. Why would you say that?"

There were two little girls skipping across the beach, hand in hand. One was tall and skinny, her long blond hair bouncing as she skipped. Her sister, a year younger, was shorter, plumper, and had black hair. They raced into the ocean and disappeared beneath the churning waves.

I squinted, concentrating on the area where they'd been, but saw nothing.

There was a small area near a line of rocks where a group of kids had gathered. They were drinking beer, I suspected, and laughing, looking like they were having a great time despite the weather.

At least until a massive wave crashed against the rocks, and drenched them, making them scramble for safety.

"What are you looking at, Astra?" Jason asked, looking out the window at the same view.

"I don't know," I admitted, and looked out the window again. "The weather is not great, it's dark, and yet that beach seems pretty happening anyway."

"Huh," was all Jason said as we watched.

The girls were back, this time wading in the ocean. The older one was a little taller, and was helping her sister out of the waves. I leaned forward, watching them. They were so cute, so innocent, so... normal.

But nothing on this stretch of beach has been what it seemed so far.

* * *

"WE'LL GET you up to speed," I told Emma.

"What are we dealing with here? Just ballpark it for me while we're waiting for everyone to finish."

"Potentially murderous undines, a mermaid with an attitude, a child ghost, and claims of a selkie, I think," I said and then took a sip of the terrible coffee. "Oh, and a dude that followed us through the Space Center, multiple fishermen that might want revenge for being hexed, and papers outlining some weird underwater casino that seems more of a pipe dream than a possible reality."

Emma laughed.

I stared at her.

She stopped laughing abruptly, her eyes wide. "I'm sorry, were you joking?"

I shook my head. "I wish I was. You guys walked into a real convoluted situation here."

Ami shushed us and turned up the volume on the television. "And I think it's about to get weirder," she said, pointing. "They're talking about Amelia."

The picture on the television flickered to a reporter standing near the shoreline of a beach and then zoomed out to show the sea.

"—Jenny Bailey reporting," the brunette reporter said into the camera. "One day ago, Amelia Arden, a local resident and employee of Elysium Condominiums, disappeared after going out on her boat. Police found her body on the beach early this morning, and they claim there was no indication of foul play. But this afternoon, local investigators changed that assessment after they searched the condominium's boat and found fish scales on the railing that matched mysterious, unidentified scales found on Amelia's body. Locals on the beach have been talking about the case all day."

The reporter disappeared off-camera and the camera panned across the beach to a crowd gathered. A blue-eyed girl with curly brown hair and a pink sweater appeared among them. The group was several yards from the camera, but the microphone managed to pick up a hint of what the young girl was telling the others.

"Amelia didn't want to go into the..." There was a pause as the girl turned her head, and the next words were unidentifiable. The girl turned again. "...but they said they'd tell on me if I didn't go."

"Who?" a member of the group asked.

The girl turned sharply, and her eyes widening at something off-camera. She broke into tears and then ran away from the crowd like something was chasing her.

No one in the group followed her.

"Could that be the ghost girl? It sounded like she knew something," Ami whispered, looking fearfully at Jason. "Please tell me that's not the little ghost girl." Her eyes welled up with tears. "We already lost our cousin. I can't handle it if a child's dead, now, too."

"Yeah, you can," Ayla told her with grim determination. "You can handle anything you have to."

"I don't think that's a girl," I said, watching the little girl. "Look." The curly-headed child was still in the background of the shot, behind the reporter. She was running straight for the ocean. "That's an undine. It has to be. Look. She's going toward the water."

As we watched the wide shot intently, the

camera angle changed and Detective Saul Marcus came into view. He waddled almost like a seal, his lips pursed, his eyes tense. The reporter turned her attention from the crowd of locals to him. "We don't believe there's any danger to the public," he said, and he looked like he meant every word he said. "This was a tragic accident, and Ms. Arden's friends were trying to do a good, but misguided, deed."

Wait.

What?

What misguided deed?

The reporter nodded but didn't ask him to elaborate. "So you think that Amelia's death was an accident."

It was, I noticed, more of a statement than a question.

"What else would it have been?" he asked, giving her a warm smile. "It was a terrible accident, and I'm sure the other girls that were with her are totally devastated." Detective Marcus looked straight into the camera. "We do wish her cousins would talk to us, but so far, they've opted to stay mum on the whole incident. If they were the last people with Ms. Arden, we believe the case is solved." He paused. "One way or another."

"Hold up," Ami snapped, looking concerned.

"Is he implying we were there?" Althea asked.

"The hell we were," Ayla snapped, her face angry.

"That's what it sounded like to me," Emma told her.

On the television, the camera panned back out to the ocean for a wide angle scenic shot. The curly-haired girl was in the ocean, swimming away from the camera. The reporter strolled in the same direction as she said, "A reminder that the ocean can be a dangerous place, and accidents can happen in the blink of an eye. This has been Jenny Bailey reporting from Cocoa Beach," she said. "Back to you in the studio, Brett—"

No one seemed concerned the girl was swimming in her pink sweater.

Ami clicked off the television.

"Well, that didn't sound good," Ayla muttered.

"Jason, tell your mother to look online," Ami said, her eyes still tearing. "See if she recognizes that girl, if that's the same girl that appeared to her."

"Okay, I think five minutes is up," Emma announced, and she pulled a chair away from the table. "Why don't you guys get Jason and me up to speed? Start at the beginning, and don't leave anything out."

CHAPTER ELEVEN

"Wow." Emma paused, looking overloaded. "Okay, so undines are fish people—fish that can turn into humans but who are essentially fish by nature," Emma said, holding up a finger. "Selkies are seal people— seals that can turn into humans but who are essentially seals. Mermaids are half fish-half human, can look fully human, but their nature is that of a mermaid and not a fish, which is something specific."

"If you guys are going to keep calling them that, at least use the proper terminology," Ayla said, annoyed. "It's fishfolk, sealfolk."

"And merfolk?" Emma asked.

Ayla nodded. "A mermaid is a female merfolk.

And she has a name, you know. We didn't meet a bunch of mermaids. We met someone named Eisheth. Just because they have animal natures doesn't mean they're not worthy of respect."

"Ah," Jason said, nodding.

Something about the situation was teasing out Ayla's previously controlled *enfant terrible* attitude. Her lively interest seemed to have transformed into something slightly darker once again. She looked up at me, her lower lip somewhat pouty as if she could sense what I was thinking.

"Okay, so undine are fishfolk," Emma said. "But a selkie is a sealfolk. I have that right?"

"Yes. Again, yes. I just said that," Ayla muttered.

"What are the other ones, then?"

"What others?" I asked.

"There are others?"

I shrugged. "None that I know of. At least not involved in this situation."

"What about the sirens?" Jason asked, tapping his finger on the table. "Didn't someone mention sirens?" No one answered. "When you were talking about Eisheth, and you didn't know if you could trust her. One of you thought she could be a siren?"

BRING YOUR BEACH OWL | 171

"Yes, but Eisheth wasn't a siren. We just thought she might be a siren."

"No sirens here," Althea added with a nod.

Emma leaned back and looked at me. "Okay, now that we're familiar with all the weird things happening here—and, honestly, this place may beat Forkbridge or Cassandra for weird—what do you think is going on? I find it hard to believe a fisherman would convince undines to drown the Hex Master protecting them from the fisherman. I mean, that just makes no sense. The fishermen are the threat."

"Are they, though?" Jason asked. "You only have the undines word for that."

"You're right. That seemed logical at the beginning, but the more that happens here, the less I understand what's happening, honestly." I looked at Ami sitting primly on the couch watching us. "What do you think? You're very quiet over there."

"I think that detective on television knows more than he's saying," she said, her eyes darting away from me toward Emma. "There was something off about his demeanor, how he talked about something Amelia did without explaining what he meant. He lied about us—he knows we weren't there. But I think there's a reason he's implying we were."

"You're the seer, right?" Emma asked.

Ami nodded like a child who knew the answer to a grown-up's question, with a plop of her head to the left, then to the right, then back to center again. "Seer, potions, death speaker and teleportation, and psychometry," she told Emma, pointing to herself, then Althea, then Ayla, and then me.

Emma narrowed her eyes at Ayla. "Everyone has one power. You have two. Why do you get two things?"

"Because I'm awesome," Ayla told her, a glint of impatience on her otherwise stoic face.

"Right. You are, indeed, awesome." Emma shifted slightly, turning to face Ayla with a direct look. "But I'm sincerely asking a question. The real reason, please?"

"We all have more than one ability," Ayla responded. "It's just that one single skill tends to be much stronger than the others. I have two, but teleportation pulls something by converting an object into energy, pulling it through the spirit world to cover the distance, and then changing the energy back into matter. Ghosts are energy." A pout formed on Ayla's face as she traced the lines on her palms and poked her fingertips together. She crossed one foot over the other, as if preparing to spend the rest of the night answering questions. "So, the two abilities are linked, kind of. Well, not kind of. They are. When someone can teleport, they also tend to be able to talk to ghosts."

I opened my eyes wide, sitting up straight. "But they also tend to be able to call ghosts." Emma and I looked at each other. "Or pull them against their will."

We all looked at Ayla.

"Why is everyone looking at me?"

Jason's cell phone rang. He held it up and stepped out onto the porch to take the call.

"You can call the little girl here," I told her. "Force it, if necessary."

Ayla's face went slack, and she shook her head. "No. I don't want to. I can't," she said, shaking her head, her eyes widening as we stared at her. "Stop looking at me like that. I don't know if I can, but I know I don't want to."

My sisters didn't know that Ayla's lessons had gotten much more in-depth, much more advanced since Aunt Gertrude showed up—and not from Aunt Gertie.

From my mother.

Mom was under the impression (likely accurate) that Gertie would have a much more substantial influence on Ayla's future, and it was up to Mom to make sure that didn't happen. So she accelerated Ayla's training as a precautionary measure, not wanting to lose too much of that integral ethical influence she still held over Ayla.

You know, the influence that had worked so well until now?

In any case, I knew Ayla had been shown things that might come in handy here—if she would try them.

"You can. Mom told you that you can," I said smoothly. "You just haven't tried."

"She's a child!" Ayla exclaimed, her voice dripping with indignant disgust.

"Why are you talking about yourself in the third person?" Althea quipped.

"I'm not talking about me, you idiot!" Ayla cast a glance at me that would have dropped me to the ground if she had a different magical power set—even with the defenses built into my uniform. "Our eldest sister wants me to reach across space and time and yank the ghost his mother was talking to! Just snatch her from wherever she is like…like…some type of soul kidnapping!"

"I know. I saw her on the news, and yes, it's

not ideal." I raised my head and fixed her with a mild stare. "She's a little girl, and she looked scared. But maybe she's alone, maybe she doesn't know where to go. Maybe you'd be helping her. She obviously wanted to get across what happened with Amelia, and she had already reached out for help. She tried telling Jason's mother and those people at the beach."

"It's her," Jason said, stepping back inside. "Mom said it's the same girl."

Ayla pulled her knees up to her chest and wrapped her arms around her legs, staring at the ceiling. "I won't do it. It's wrong."

As we all stared at Ayla, the room fell silent. We seemed to wait for someone to approach her, for someone to volunteer to persuade her to do what the rest of us, judging by our expressions, already knew needed to be done.

"Okay. No problem. They're your powers. You have an ultimate right to control what you do with them and what you don't. I can't make you do anything you don't want to do or that you don't believe in, Ayla," I said, tilting my head. She raised her head and looked at me with relief. "Let's just go to the police and tell them what we know. They'll take care of it," I told her.

Ayla's head snapped back. She looked at me as

if I'd just grown a vampire head of out my nose. "You can't be serious."

"Well, it's not my preferred method of dealing with this, but what choice do we have? The police announced to the entire viewing area that we were with Amelia when she died. How easy do you think it will be getting other leads now? Better just to tell the police what we know—at least the info we can share with them—and leave it to them to solve."

"I don't trust them, and I know you don't," she snapped at me. The tension crackled between us as she seemed to work through her options, and then she relaxed her posture. "And I know what you're doing, too. That reverse psychology stuff won't work on me, big sister. I won't do it."

"Ayla, honestly, I don't see any other choice," Jason said, frowning. "She disappeared, and my mother is sure she had more to say. And Astra is right. She's tried to reach out for help *twice* now if we count that conversation with those people on the beach. What if she disappeared because someone else pulled her across space and time? The people in this room are not the only magic users involved. What if someone not so concerned for her—"

"Oh, come on, dude—you're not even a witch,"

Ayla said. "Quit talking about things you don't understand. You don't get an opinion. You—"

"I'm a teacher. I know what a scared child looks like," Jason responded, cutting her off gently. "That little girl was scared, and both times we've seen her? She was very much alone."

This was so patently true that it stopped Ayla for a moment, freezing her anger as she worked through what Jason said. Then, finally, she seemed to dismiss his rationale. "Look, you don't *know*. And what you're asking me to do? It's just wrong. Besides, even if it wasn't? I don't know anything about that. I don't know how to do it," Ayla said, her lips quivering.

"You don't know how to do what?" Emma asked. "And why do you keep telling yourself you don't know? Ayla, you figured out how to break a generational family curse all on your own. I don't buy that you don't know—and even if that's true, I don't buy that you couldn't figure it out if you needed to."

Ayla looked at her.

"Tell yourself you don't know how, and you're right. You don't."

"But what if I hurt her?" Ayla whispered, her eyes wet with unshed tears.

"Let us help you then," I told Ayla. "I know

some things. And Ami knows a lot of other things. And Althea, well, I'm surprised Althea's brain doesn't explode considering all the things she knows."

Ayla's face softened as she half-smiled, making her look slightly more confident in the situation presenting itself and her ability to navigate it. However, this half-smile soon fell away. She closed her eyes, and her brow furrowed. The muscles in her arms twitched as she clenched her fists.

Finally, she nodded.

And with a half-hour of preparation, we did help her.

And she was wrong.

She could do it.

We just weren't expecting to teleport a shark to the center of the hotel room.

* * *

NONE of us had ever seen a great white shark before. But somehow, we all knew what we were looking at was a great white shark—and this one was in trouble. It was flopping around on the red carpet, its gills opening and closing as it gasped for air, and it seemed to glow violet like a freshly painted car in the sun.

"Get water! Oh, no, oh no!" Ayla yelled, leaning down to pick it up.

"Ayla!" Jason said sharply. "Not only can you hurt it, but it could also hurt you. Those teeth are razor sharp!"

My sister's expression was pained and helpless. "What do I do?" She looked down at the fish. "I am so sorry! I thought you were a ghost, but you're not a ghost! I am so sorry!"

Ami grabbed a jug of water and poured it over the fierce-looking fish—which was gasping for air and beating its tail wildly as it flopped around. "Oh, crap," she said, mortified. "Maybe I should have put it in the jug? Why did I do that?"

"It's too big to fit in the jug, and you panicked," I told her as I racked my brain on how to get the young shark to safety. "It happens." If the shark was an undine, it should be able to transform into an air-breathing humanoid with a sustained thought. Despite this, the five-foot great white flopped helplessly, its eyes wild.

"Astra, what do we do?" Althea asked.

Emma grabbed a glass from the table and ran to the kitchen. "I got it!"

"Not a glass. Fill up the bathtub!" Ayla told

Althea. "It's okay, we'll get you in some water. That's right. You're okay. Take it easy."

"Astra, that's a shark," Jason told me, his voice low. "There are none in captivity because they're so difficult to hold and house. While some fish can pump water in and out of their gills using their mouths, sharks like the great white need to be constantly in motion for water to enter their gills. It—she—has to be constantly moving."

"Or?"

"They weaken and struggle to breathe. Then they suffocate."

The immense fish (for a hotel room) was flopping around, its eyes dazed, trying to find oxygen. I tried to gently grasp its tail to stop it from struggling, but the skin was slimy, and it twisted from my grip. "Why don't you join us on two legs?" I asked her gently. "Come on, just transform. We all know who you are."

The shark stared back at me, its eyes reflecting its terror.

I sighed in frustration.

I could not grab this fish with my hands, not without hurting it.

I took a pebble from my tool belt and whispered *liquidum*. A water globe—just a ball of churning water not contained within anything—

the size of an average crystal ball appeared in the palm of my hand.

"What is that?" Emma asked.

"Fish handcuffs, I guess," I told her as I slowly tapped it to make it bigger, and bigger, and then bigger still. "There are a lot of paranormals that live in fresh and saltwater, and some of them can't breathe air." The ball of water churned, and the room smelled like the sea. "We still had to take them into custody and get them back to Impy City. So this is how we did it."

"Why isn't she changing, though?" Ayla asked, her voice shaking with terror and regret. "If this is the girl, why isn't she changing?"

"She's just frightened, that's all," I told Ayla, my voice soothing both for Ayla's benefit and the young great white shark. "She's defenseless in her human form," I guessed, tapping the ball to grow larger and lowering it slowly toward the shark. "At least in this form, she has her teeth."

Finally, the magical water ball grew to about five feet across, and I thanked the Ministry's object magicians that they remembered to cast spells to lighten the object. There were hundreds of gallons of water making up the globe, weighing around eight pounds per gallon.

Without magical density spells, I could never lift the thing.

I lowered the surging, frothing circle of magical water to the carpet and gently touched it to the shark. The water reached out toward the shark and sucked it in like a vacuum, slurping the gasping fish up into the massive water ball. The water ball recalculated the needed space a few seconds later and popped out, doubling in size.

It now took up roughly half the space in the large hotel room.

The shark swam around the globe, frantic, for just a moment before pausing near the side. It blinked. Then, with a swish of its tail, the shark thrust its head out, looked at me, and pulled its head back in. It blinked again.

"You're okay, I promise," I whispered.

The fish stared back, looking frightened, but its color was coming back, and it appeared in less distress than it had been.

"You really stole—I'm sorry, appropriated—some weird stuff from the military, didn't you?" Emma murmured, her eyes wide.

"It's not going to be able to breathe," Jason said. "It's not moving. The area is too small and—"

"It can breathe just fine now," I said gently,

quietly, reaching out toward the great white and bopping it affectionately on the nose. Ripples danced across the water's surface as the sphere accommodated my hand, but the ball kept its form. "This ball of water can keep a water-breathing creature alive for days. It knows exactly what she needs. If you look closely, you can see the water is flowing past her. She's fine." I removed my hand. "How're you doing in there?"

"Fine," the fish said in a high-pitched, childlike voice. "But where is there? And who are you? Are you the bad people?"

"No, we're good people," Jason said, crossing his arms and leaning back against the wall. "We won't hurt you, little one. We're friends of Amelia, and we wanted to ask you some questions about what happened to her."

"I don't know. Are they friends, too?" The little fish swam around the sphere, peering toward me.

"None of us will hurt you," I said. "Are there bad people where you're from?"

"Everyone is bad," she said. "The people who took me. The other people. They're all bad. Even the good people are bad. The bad people," the young shark shuddered, "are everywhere."

CHAPTER TWELVE

The shark was clearly not a ghost.

I stared back at the young great white shark in the magical globe tank. Its eyes— her eyes—were cold and unblinking. Her razor sharp teeth were just barely visible through her slightly open mouth. The shark's body moved, fierce and energetic as if swimming a great distance at a brisk pace. The magic of the globe, though, pushed the water in a continuous current so that, despite the shark's swimming effort, she remained suspended.

"It's going to be much easier for us to talk if you take your human form," I told her. "It's getting pretty humid in this room. How about coming out?"

She didn't respond.

I knew she was petrified.

She had to be thinking about all the steps she'd taken to find aid, only to be ripped across time and space and plopped into a water ball in a shabby hotel room. Jason, Emma, and my sisters were transfixed, looking at the shark while doing their best to look non-threatening.

I'd hoped by providing the shark a relatively safe space to engage with her surroundings, she'd see we didn't want to harm her. I reached out slowly, my gloved hand hovering over the water globe—

"Astra!" Ami shouted. "She could bite you!"

"The gloves will protect me," I responded calmly. "She can't hurt me."

I stopped mid-reach as her muscular body tensed.

It didn't appear we were there yet.

She was so afraid. She was unsure. And she looked more than a little lost.

I shook my head, pulled my hand back, and cleared my throat. "You're safe in that magic water globe, but it's taking up almost half the room, and it's going to be difficult for us two-legged folks to navigate around the room."

Her gills expanded and contracted.

"It'll be easier for everyone if you come out."

I waited.

She stared.

"You're not afraid of me," she finally said, her voice small.

"No," I told her. "I don't think you mean us harm any more than we mean you harm."

The young shark didn't take her eyes from my face, but her mouth opened slightly wider, and her gills seemed to flex. Significant ripples appeared in the water, waves that eventually made their way to the edge of the globe. "No, thank you. I'll stay in here, please." Her voice was thin, shaky, and very young.

"What's your name?"

"Mitzi."

"Why not come out?"

"I can't," she said finally, her voice slightly stronger. "I can't do that."

"Why not?"

Long pause. "Because as soon as you see me in my human form, you're going to capture me."

"That's certainly not our intention, not at all. So why would you think we would want to capture you?" I asked.

Ayla snorted. "Most ironic question ever."

She was right. I knew it was a confusing

question even as it left my lips—though leave it to Ayla to comment on how ridiculous it was.

I had captured the juvenile great white. She was contained in the transport sphere. There was no way for her to leave the water ball unless I let her out. And yet...

I sensed she meant something else, something different.

"Because that's what you do!" she said. "You kill sharks! You take them, and they die! You trick them and make them think there's a fish to eat and then you take them! You hunters want us all dead!"

"We mean you no harm. We're not going to kill you," I told her. "I promise."

She looked at Jason. "You're going to put me in a tank. I know how you do things. You're going to take me somewhere and make me do tricks for people to see. Or put me in a glass box. Or cut off my fins." Her eyes shifted to me momentarily and then back to the others in the room. "And then I'll never see my mom again."

It could strike someone as odd, seeing a great white shark frightened by humans—but their lack of cute and cuddliness had led to a host of practices by humans that could only be considered shark atrocities. If you looked at them from the perspective of sharks, at least.

It was odd, too. As top predators, their disappearance would disrupt *entire* ocean ecosystems, and some people know it. In 1999, the United Nations created the International Plan of Action for the Conservation and Management of Sharks. The problem?

No country is forced to participate, and protections for sharks varied wildly from complete all the way to none.

"I promise—we want to help you," I told her.

Again.

Still not knowing what I could do to help.

She looked at Jason again, fear in her unblinking eyes. "You're a hunter," she said. She said the words in a matter-of-fact tone of voice, almost as if she were describing how the sun rose in the east and water tasted salty. "Mama told me to stay away from you and to stay with Amelia. Because you're hunters."

He shook his head. "I am not a hunter. I am a teacher."

Mitzi looked at him like he was the biggest idiot in the world. "You're a hunter," she repeated. She turned to me. "You're not a hunter, but you're with him, so you're helping the hunters."

I looked at Jason. The little shark seemed fixated on him as potentially threatening—but not as much on the rest of us.

She feared him because he was a man.

"No," I told her. "I'm not. I've spent a lot of time with Jason. I promise he's not a hunter. I've never seen him harm anything or anyone in all the time I've known him. Just because he's a man doesn't mean he's a hunter."

"In fact, I'm here because you reached out to my mother," Jason said, slowly stepping forward. "She thought you were a ghost because your spirit came to find her and talk to her. She called me so I could come down here and tell Astra you needed her help."

"The spirit light lady?" the little shark asked, seeming to perk up. "Your mama is the spirit light lady in the spirit light town?" Slowly, a metamorphosis took place before our eyes, and the shark became a girl. The same little girl we saw on the news report. Mitzi floated in the water, seemingly unconcerned there was no air. "She said she would send help for Astra, who was already helping." She turned in the ball of water and stared at me. "Are you the Astra?"

"That's my name, yes. Just Astra. It's not a title."

"You're Amelia's cousin?"

"All of us are," I said, gesturing to my sisters, who nodded. "We're not hunters, and Jason is not a hunter," I told the girl. "We're here to help."

"My name is Mitzi," she said again, her mouth making bubbles in the water. "And no one helps, you know. Even if they try, they die. The hunters get them."

Jason opened his mouth to protest, but a sharp look from me silenced him. I would not argue that point with this young girl at this moment. We needed her to feel comfortable, we needed her to talk, and we needed to know who the hunters were.

And we needed to get her out of the gigantic water ball.

It was going from humid to icky in here.

"I wasn't supposed to be here," she said. She paused. "I'm not supposed to be here. If my mom finds out I'm here, she's going to be very upset with me."

"Where are you supposed to be?" I asked.

"I have to get to the ocean and stay out from the shore. Far back."

"Why?"

"I'm supposed to be there. Mom said it's safer there. I can only—" Mitzi stopped and looked panicked. "I have to go to the ocean. That's where I should be."

"Why does your mom think that's safer than here?"

Mitzi fell silent.

I looked at her for a long moment. Her eyes were steady and almost pleading.

Finally, I nodded, took off my gloves, and held out my exposed, unprotected hands to her—it would, I hoped, get across that I trusted her not to hurt me. She studied my fingers for a long time, and then a large ripple in the water made its way around the globe and seemed to reach out toward me. "Take my hands. Let us help you."

"You're really not a hunter?" she asked, her little voice full of doubt.

"I am not," I told her. "I swear. Please, Mitzi—trust me."

"Because hunters kill sharks," she reminded me. Mitzi's eyes wandered over each one of us and then returned to me. "Can I see your hands?"

I put my hands into the water, bare and exposed. It was nerve-racking just a bit, I'll admit —she could turn back into a shark and bite me before I could pull them to safety. My body tensed as I was barraged with an onslaught of images—water has a long memory, and this water had transported many, many water-creatures to Imperatorial City. I struggled to maintain my calm.

But then Mitzi reached out with her tiny hand and pressed her fingers against mine to feel my skin. She looked directly into my eyes. "You don't have a knife?" she asked. "You promise?"

"I promise."

"You won't take me away?"

"I won't take you away."

* * *

THE CHILD, her clothes dripping wet, followed me around the room like a puppy. It always impressed me that ancient magic took modesty into account—though I still don't understand how shapeshifters keep their clothes.

We sat down next to each other.

Mitzi reached out and stroked my face, then pushed closer until her wet hair brushed my lips. Again, I had the familiar sense of being inside another person's head, but instead of discovering an adult's experiences, her mind opened and a flood of childhood images—for a fish—rushed by.

Yes, she was a child.

But she was also a great white shark.

Sharks are mysterious creatures, and great whites are the most mysterious of all. Impossible to hold in captivity, challenging to study. We know some things, but not many.

I did know that sharks (non-undine sharks) can't make any noise, so they communicate through body language. When two great whites "talk" to each other, they may open their jaws, nod their heads, and arch their bodies. When two sharks pursue the same prey, they might slap each other to deter the other from interfering.

This communication is critical—great whites try to avoid fights as much as possible since a single bite can be fatal.

This critical communication lesson appeared to be the thing Mitzi's mother was trying to teach her when the hunters came upon them.

A difference, I noted, between an undine great white and a "regular" great white. When great white shark pups are born, they immediately swim away from their mothers, fully prepared to care for themselves.

Undine great whites take motherhood much more seriously.

I shared the panicked, terrifying images with her, feeling her tense at the memory. It was incredibly unpleasant, but I watched and hoped I could get a glimpse of the "hunters" that had taken Mitzi's mother.

With Mitzi below water and the hunters above, it was impossible. I did see letters on the side of the blue boat, though: FIRET. There may have been more, but I couldn't make it out.

I gratefully finished the slide show of meaningful images in my mind's eye and then broke contact with the girl. Mitzi's deep blue eyes grew wide for a moment, as if she had been reading my mind, too. "What is it?"

She said, in a child's "I know everything" voice, "You don't know who the hunters are. You were trying to see them because you don't know who they are."

"You know that just by touching Astra?" Jason asked, surprised.

The girl met his eyes for a moment, then her gaze fluttered around the room. "I am undine. I have telepathic and hydrokinetic powers," she told him. "I can hear the thoughts of every living thing, human or nonhuman, on the whole planet. But not all at once. That would make my head hurt a lot." She looked down shyly. "And only when I'm not scared. When I'm scared, it doesn't work very well. And I try to avoid listening to humans. It's too distracting, and some of the thoughts are bad." She shuddered. "I don't like scary people."

As a child, I'd been fascinated by the claims of the undine great white's existence—so intelligent and graceful, so beautiful and terrible that certain death awaited those who dared to engage one.

Now, sitting next to Mitzi, she seemed less beautiful and terrible and more lost little girl that needed help.

"Can you not hear the hunters?" I asked.

"They're not hiding," Mitzi said. "But they're not...thinking loudly?" Her face screwed up in concentration. "I feel their thoughts, but they don't feel like...like human thoughts. They're not very loud. So I think they're thinking about not thinking."

"Mitzi, do you know where your mom is?" I asked. "Can you hear her thoughts?" I didn't know the little girl's paranormal capabilities. As I've said, great white sharks were mysterious creatures, and little is known about their behavior or biology. Undine great white sharks?

Even more mysterious.

Mitzi shook her head. "She said the hunters were coming, and we had to get away from Cocoa Beach. Mom told me to get to the ocean if something happened to her. So I did, even after they took her. And I've stayed there. Waiting." She blushed. "Well, until you brought me here."

"Astra, what did you see when you touched Mitzi?" Ami's eyes were closed, her hands on her knees as though she were meditating. "Because I see a boat. A blue boat with three men aboard." She shuddered. "I don't recognize any of them." She opened her eyes. "But then again, I didn't see the man at the Space Center. I wouldn't recognize it if it was him. Only you saw him."

"I saw a blue boat, too," I told her. "FIRET? It was in white on the side, but I don't know if that was the full name—"

"Firethorn," she responded.

"As in Firethorn Development Corporation," Althea said dryly. "Why am I not surprised?"

"Who's the Firethorn Development Corporation?" Emma looked first at Althea, then Ami, and finally at Althea. "And if you're the only person who saw the mysterious guy following you, why don't you just grab Ami's hand and peek in on whatever visions she's having?"

I had no time to answer before something crashed into the balcony.

Mitzi screamed.

* * *

ARCHIE FLEW IN, all feathers and fury, as soon as Jason opened the sliding door.

"IF YOU WERE ALL MEETING IN HERE, YOU COULD HAVE LEFT THE PATIO DOOR OPEN!" Archie shouted in a tone that brooked no opposition or argument. "I've been hovering outside that stupid window for twenty minutes, hoping you or Jason would look out!"

"Why didn't you just land and tap on the window?" I asked, exasperated.

"Have you looked at this hotel? How did I know what you and the fickle middle school ladies' man were doing in this rent-by-the-hour bawdy house by the sea?"

My boyfriend blinked. "I can hear him. And it's not a bawdy house. It's a hotel," Jason muttered.

"That rents by the hour!"

"It does not." Jason sounded uncharacteristically testy.

"Archie, you were the one that stormed off, not me. I didn't leave the window open because I thought you'd be smart enough to tap on the glass," I told him incredulously, my arm around the young girl. "If you decided you wanted to be in my presence again, anyway—which, frankly, after the way you flew off? Wasn't a given."

"I swear, you two are like an old married couple," Ayla murmured.

I shot a scathing look at Ayla, leaned back on the couch, and fixed my gaze on Archie. "Well? Did you come here just to insult me, or did you have something to report?"

"What am I, your servant?" He glared back. "You know, I have never killed a witch, but I have read many obituaries with smug pleasure."

"That's a Clarence Darrow quote. Well," I said, holding out my hand moving it diagonally, "it was almost a Clarence Darrow quote."

"He got it from me, you idiot—"

"Okay, stop it," Althea snapped. "Both of you. The merciless insult-flinging is amusing sometimes, but not at the moment. Do either of you remember what happened at Yule? Do you really want the gods to show up here, too? Because I think we have enough problems already between our cousin and the baby shark."

"If Jason and I can hear Archie, does that mean this is a star card case?" Emma asked, eyeing me thoughtfully. "I lose track of all the magical rules and regulations."

"We haven't seen one, no," I responded, thinking back to everything that transpired. I looked at Ami. "Did you do any readings we don't know about?"

"Tons, but not with a glowy star card."

"Is this really the most important thing we need to figure out?" Ayla's bright stare blinked at us from the corner. "Why Jason and Emma can hear Archie? Maybe Astra's powers are getting stronger. Maybe Athena decided to let them hear to make everything easier on Astra. Maybe Archie's changing. Who cares? I swear, you guys get distracted by the weirdest things."

"That's not what this is," Emma disagreed. "In an investigation, you never know what's important, and you always mark things that are different. This is different."

"The more you deal with the paranormal, the more you're probably attuned to it." Althea shrugged. "People that don't believe in the paranormal can't see any of what we see and half the time don't even notice us even though we're right in front of them. Ayla's right. I don't think it's important."

Emma held up her hands as if she was giving up the debate. "So Archie's like Tinkerbell? If we believe, we can hear him?" She chuckled. "Sure, we'll go with that for now."

"Like I'm Tinkerbell?" The owl's black eyes

glittered. "Like I'm Puff, the magic dragon? Like I'm Rainbow Bright?"

"Like, you're spasmodic, dude." Ayla leaned down toward Archie and pointed. "You have the most mercurial personality of anyone I have ever met, and I was raised by Minerva Arden, so that's saying something. But, take it down a notch. And you called Jason fickle?"

"Who's that?" the owl asked, his unrelenting gaze fixed on Mitzi—who still clung to my arm, her eyes wide. "Is that a child?" He glared at Jason. "Did you two bend space-time and have some godchild in the bawdy house while I was off working on the case?"

"No!" we shouted simultaneously.

"Oh, wow. Archie. Dude." Ayla shook her head in disappointment and then jumped up from the bed where she'd been sitting. Then, shuddering, she mumbled, "Gross."

"It's happened before!" he snapped.

I explained as briefly as I could who Mitzi was (through clenched teeth) and what she'd said, adding what else we knew so far. "We'd just realized the boat that took Mitzi's mother had the same name as the corporation that Amelia was looking into, Firethorn Development Corporation. Well, Firethorn," I explained, trying to ignore Archie's horrible attitude. "There were three men on the boat. Ami saw them, but my view was through Mitzi's eyes in the water. So I couldn't see who was on the boat."

"Again," Emma interrupted, jerking her head toward Ami. "Grab Ami's hand. Take a look."

It seemed logical. So logical that anyone in that room might be wondering why I hadn't thought of it before. The fundamental truth was that I had worked alone in the military, as had all of the soldiers in my division. Even though I was a Decanus and led legionaries, we were still taught to depend on ourselves in battle and trust no one in the field.

Working together didn't come instinctively for me.

I'd gotten better at it since working with Emma, I thought as I stood up, Mitzi still clinging to my side like a barnacle—but clearly, I still had a long way to go.

"Ready?" She nodded.

I took her hand in mine, closed my eyes, and saw the sights she had seen. The guy I'd seen at the Space Center was driving the boat and smiling as if he enjoyed the sensation of the wind in his hair, the sun on his skin, and the waves slamming against the hull. He might have been any Floridian enjoying a day at the beach.

The other two I didn't recognize.

The visuals then shifted, like ripples in a roiled pond. The colors changed, and the edges became more pronounced.

"This is new," Ami whispered. "I haven't seen this."

A fourth man climbed up from the cabin and stood on deck, a bamboo-handled harpoon in his hand. I'd know that man anywhere.

Ami gasped. "Is that—"

"It is."

"Who is it?" Emma asked, her voice sounding far away.

Detective Saul Marcus.

CHAPTER THIRTEEN

*I*f you were born in the African deserts of the Sahara, then moved to the Pacific Northwest, then back to the desert, you'd get used to change. You'd learn that change isn't always a bad thing. You'd know to expect the unexpected and adjust, sometimes with staggering speed. As much as people complain about change, things feel normal faster than people expect.

The world underwater was a world, though. For people above the waterline, below was always alien. Always different. It was fast, fluid, and constantly changing—and yet it was the same, always the same.

Here on the surface, the world kept turning,

the seasons changing, the snow melting, the leaves withering, the rain falling, the light shining on the green grass of early spring at the farm.

Things didn't change beneath the ocean unless something—or someone—changed it.

I glanced out the window. "Looks like the storm is letting up." I turned to Mitzi, curious. "What do you know about Eisheth, the mermaid?"

The child smiled brightly. "You've met her," she said with joy. "She's the one who gets the wounded undine and brings them to Elysium."

"What? What do you mean?"

"She's like a fish goddess, kind of. She transports hurt fishfolk to safety sometimes." Althea offered Mitzi a glass of water, which she accepted. "She's an ancient water elemental, you know—older than most of the others in the ocean. Amelia told me Eisheth is not happy with the fish hospital, though," Mitzi said after a pause.

"Why not?"

Mitzi shrugged.

I watched Ami as she shuffled her tarot cards. She laid them out, then reshuffled, and then laid them out again. Over and over, like she was searching for an answer that refused to appear. My sister was so focused, her eyes narrowed in concentration, that she didn't notice everyone in the room watching her silently as she gazed at the images, thinking.

"Out with it. What's bothering you?" Althea asked.

"The Lovers card has appeared multiple times," Ami said. She tapped the card with her finger. "Over and over, again and again. That's no accident. I don't know what it means, but so far, there's nothing about this situation that seems to relate to it. At least not that I know of." She looked up. "But that card is trying to tell me something."

I leaned against the wall, one hand on a hip. "Does anyone have any idea if there was anyone Amelia was interested in? Or had been involved with?"

"How would we know?" Ayla responded. "We never go anywhere, we never do anything, and we never talk to anyone that isn't priestessed to Athena. Even family."

"We were in her house, Ayla. Did you see any pictures of anyone that might indicate a romantic relationship? Roses in a vase, anything like that?"

"There were no pictures on her walls," Althea answered. "Nothing by her bedside, either. There were no love letters, no photos on her nightstand or her bureau."

"Amelia was a loner," Mitzi added.

Ami stared at the cards. "I don't know what it is, but I don't think she was. I don't think she was as much of a loner as you think, Mitzi." Ami looked up at the little girl. "Wait. Why do you think she was a loner?"

"She always went out on the boat alone. No one ever went out with her."

Amelia was always alone on that huge boat.

And yet I trusted Ami's cards.

If something was nagging at my sister, there was a reason for it.

"We need to go back to the condo," I said, glancing at Emma. "We missed something. Well, we probably missed a lot of things. We didn't really know what to look for when we were there before, and I could use your fresh eyes on the place."

Ami packed up the cards and rose. She looked at me. "If it's okay with you, I'll come back and cast the cards again in the apartment. Maybe I can get a better idea if I'm in the place where Amelia lived instead of this—"

"Bawdy house?" Archie asked helpfully.

"But I can't go there!" Mitzi cried out, her

lower lip jutting out in a frightened pout. She looked panicked by the thought, her gray eyes wide as she stared at me. "I can't go there. It's too dangerous. Mama told me it's way dangerous and I have to stay away from there. Especially there."

Althea tousled her hair. "Ayla and I will stay here with you, kid."

Emma and I glanced at one another in that way we had when something significant was said, but we weren't sure why we thought it was.

"Mitzi—you're an undine, and that's an undine sanctuary. So why would that place be dangerous for you?" I asked the young shark-shifter. "Isn't it supposed to be someplace safe for people like you?"

"It is, but it's not," she answered confusingly. "It's supposed to be, but it's not. I just can't go there."

"If you know something about the Elysium Condos, Mitzi, tell us," I told her. "We're trying to help."

She struggled, her face tense, and then shook her head, tears in her eyes. "I can't. I don't know why Mama told me to stay away from there. I don't know because she didn't tell me. But I know it's a bad place now."

* * *

"How did she communicate with my mother?" Jason asked quietly as we crossed the street. My sisters (other than Ami) stayed in the hotel room with Mitzi—who was not happy that I was leaving. I had confidence they could protect her if someone showed up at the hotel, but I didn't see why anyone would. Jason and Emma came along with Ami and me to Amelia's condo. "Without being a ghost, I mean."

"Astral projection," Ami explained. "With astral projection, a person can leave their body and travel to another place. They do it all the time in the ocean—I've even heard stories of undines jumping from body to body the way hermit crabs trade shells. It's a side effect of water elemental magic." She tucked her hair behind her ear. "Anyone—even humans—can do it when they're in a trance, but I don't know all of the details. I've never done it, so I can't explain it all to you."

Jason looked surprised. "You've never done it?"

Ami shook her head. "It leaves the body defenseless, and there's a risk the silver cord will snap if someone goes too far or is gone too long. So it can be dangerous."

"The silver cord is?" Jason asked, his expression baffled.

"Sorry." Ami smiled. "It's how your soul is connected to your body."

Jason, Ami, Emma, and I walked to the dark parking lot in front of the yellow condo building. A scrawny birch tree stretched out over the blacktop, its branches drooping lower than the others. Behind them, rays of moonlight streamed through the dissipating clouds.

I spotted our original parking spot, now occupied, and flashed back to the woman determined I would not park there. A work truck, beige in color and clean enough not to be dirty, took up the space. It was parked facing away from the building, its windows tinted and opaque from the outside.

Suddenly, the truck's driver's door opened.

The cab was big, and so was the man sitting in the driver's seat. Well, sort of. He was short, wide, and had a round belly. His red baseball cap proclaimed his love of the Cincinnati Reds, and he wore a white T-shirt with a logo I couldn't quite see.

As he turned to get out, I realized it was a cartoon of a pirate ship.

"Hide!" I hissed and raced to crouch behind my Jeep. The thundering (and not at all subtle) steps of Jason, Emma, and Ami echoed through the lot as they followed.

Well, probably not Emma.

Emma was a police detective; she knew how to sneak.

The teacher and the tarot card reader?

Sneaking was not their forte.

The guy in the vehicle resembled the man I saw earlier today near the pier, retrieving something from the water with his hands. I couldn't be sure it was the same man, but I was more confident than not. "Don't let him see you," I whispered.

The truck was parked next to a pile of discarded deck planks at the back of the lot that looked like they had been left over from some home improvement project. I didn't remember them being there before—the planks were stacked almost to the truck's height and blocked the parking lot's view of the beach.

"What is it?" Jason asked in a low voice. "Why do you think—?"

"Shh!" Emma hissed at him.

He flipped down a large lever on the side of the door, opened the door even further, and stepped out. He looked in our direction but didn't move. "Well, now, that's a pretty Jeep," he said to himself, his voice cheerful. "I like black Jeeps. Not like you, old Bertha." He walked around to the back, reached into the open bed, and pulled out the pail I'd seen him with earlier today. "Not that you're not a good girl, but you sure ain't pretty like that Jeep over there. Though I guess it's my fault you always smell like fish."

He returned to the front of the truck, reached inside, and turned off the lights. His keys fell to the ground as he was doing so. He knelt down to get them, then groaned as he drew back up. "I'm getting too old for this, Bertha," the man told his boring-colored truck. "These problems need to end soon. I'm telling you, I'm too old for this."

The man's words to his truck had a mournful tone to them. The heavy man grunted as he drew pails from the truck bed. He then walked around the truck, between the decking stack, and toward the beach.

* * *

"COME ON," I whispered, slipping out from behind the Jeep. "I saw that man grabbing something out of the ocean earlier today, right next to the condo's boat. I want to know what he's doing."

"Astra, those pails he's got are heavy," Emma pointed out.

"Yeah, I was just going to say. I don't think he's pulling something out of the ocean," Jason said as we hurried across the parking lot toward the man's truck. "I think he's bringing something *to* the ocean."

Ami peeked around the decking and waved us on. "We'll know soon enough."

We hurried around the beige truck to the back, Ami and Jason skirting the sides, me and Emma crouching low. The work truck was parked in shadow, but the moon—huge white and full—shone down into the parking lot. I glanced up at the sky. It was quickly transitioning to a dark, clear night, in stark contrast to the earlier storm.

We reached the back of the truck, the pails clanking as the man walked down the slope toward the beach. I peeked in the truck bed but saw nothing that would give me a clue what the man was up to.

We stepped onto the beach and attempted to follow the man casually. He was walking across the sand toward the dock, where I'd first seen him. We had to take our steps slowly to keep a safe, non-threatening distance from him, but once on the beach, there was really no way for us to sneak or hide.

As if red cap sensed us, he stopped, turned around, and stared. "Hey."

I lifted my hand. "Hello. Nice night for a walk."

He looked around. "No, it's not. Everything's wet."

The man stood in front of us, holding a pail in each hand and looking at us with a puzzled expression on his face. The sun and years of hard work had lined his narrow face, which was framed by gray hair, limp as if in need of a wash. He had a sharp, slightly too long nose bookended by chubby cheeks.

"That was some storm, huh?" Jason said, nodding.

"It's Florida," he said as if that explained everything about the weather. "What are you doing out here?" The way he looked at us made me slightly uncomfortable; it was as if we were trespassing on his private beach. He glanced back at the way he had come to confirm that it was still clear and then turned his attention to us once again.

"It's a public beach. And I could ask you the same thing," I said.

"I live here." He shifted the pails in his hands. "What are you doing?" he demanded again, a little more insistently this time.

I stared at him. "Taking a walk on the beach?" I stepped closer to him to better look at the pails he held behind him like he was their shield. "What are the buckets for? Are you going night fishing for something?" A tiny gray face popped out of the pail water and blinked at me.

I'm embarrassed to say I jumped.

And maybe squeaked a tiny little bit.

"Holy sea urchin, what are those?" Emma breathed, staring.

"None of your business," the man snapped, yanking the pails behind him.

"Those are sharks," Jason said. "That's a shark face."

"They are not," the man told him, looking worried.

I peered into the pail again. "They are, too. They're baby sharks." Another face popped out, then another. They glared up at me, expressionless. Finally, one blinked and then disappeared back into the murky water. They were much smaller than a newborn great white would be, but their faces were unmistakably shark-like.

The man grabbed the pails more tightly, turned around, and walked away from us. "I'm taking them to their home. Where they belong. Why don't you go home where you belong? That way, everyone's where they should be. Good night!"

"Why are they in a pail?" I demanded, taking another step toward him. "Where did you get them?"

He shook his head as he trudged across the beach. "I don't know who you are, or what you want, or why you're bothering me, but I need to get these babies in the ocean. I don't have time for your questions. So unless you're a game warden," he called over his shoulder as he walked away, "leave me alone."

I stared at his retreating back. "What is with this place and sharks?"

"Astra," Ami whispered. She pointed toward the waves. "Look. Is that Eisheth?" I followed my sister's pointing finger and saw a pale woman bobbing in the waves. She swam toward the man,

218 | LEANNE LEEDS

who appeared to be oblivious to her presence as he patiently made his way toward the dock, his pails clanking.

I stood there, admiring how the creature moved through the water with such grace and speed, my gaze fixed on Eisheth until she dove. When the mermaid's upper body once again emerged from the water, a small shark was dangling between two of her fingers. She carefully handed it to the man, who placed it in one of the pails. He reached into the other and carefully dropped the baby sharks he'd brought into the ocean alongside her.

"Wow," Jason breathed, stunned at what he was witnessing. "I don't even know what's happening, but that's a mermaid. So, wow."

"You said it," Emma agreed.

Eisheth rose up from the water, her scaled hips visible, and turned toward the four of us. "Now you see what's at stake," she called out, her voice strong and clear in the night air as she bobbed oddly high above the water. "Some shape-shifters have turned on the natural world, the natural order of things. The waves are my home, and I'll fight to protect all that live here, all that is meant to be here." She paused and stared at each of us in turn. "But I cannot turn against my own."

She seemed to stare directly at me for a long moment as if willing me to understand. "Even when they turn against the ocean itself."

She dove into the water and disappeared.

"That was…" Jason shook his head, stunned.

Ami turned to me. "She wants us to do something about the sharks," she said, looking at me. "I think. I don't know." Ami sighed. "Something's happening, and she can't stop it directly. I don't think she can even tell us, exactly."

"Yes, I think you're right," I replied simply.

"She's a mermaid. If she can't stop it, what can we do?"

"I don't know."

Jason's turned to look at my sister and then pointed down at her feet. "Hey, Ami? You dropped a card."

The stiff rectangle of paper was flipped over on the sand in front of Ami's shoes. "The Lover's Card," she whispered. She picked it up and examined it. Then, suddenly, she looked up at me. "You don't think Amelia and Eisheth were in a relationship, do you? Like, a romantic one?"

"Of course they were," the man with the pails said as he trudged back up to where we were standing. He set the buckets down carefully, shaking his head in exasperation. However, his tone was much friendlier than it had been. "We all know that. If you know Eisheth well enough for her to actually speak to you, how do you not know that?"

"My sister and I are Amelia's cousins, but we didn't know her very well. We've only met Eisheth once, so I wouldn't say we know her well, either," I explained, my tone apologetic and respectful. "My name is Astra, and this is my sister Ami. That's my friend Emma," I said, gesturing to the detective without mentioning she was a detective. "The man behind her is Jason."

"Nice to meet you all," the man nodded. He stopped, glanced behind me, and scanned the area. Once assured we were alone, he said, "My name is Joe Tiburon. I work at the building over there doing maintenance. Among other things, now." He jerked his chin back toward the yellow building. "Elysium's been changing of late, so I do what I can." He squinted. "You're witches, aren't you?"

I nodded. "Ami and I. Are you an undine?"

Joe looked toward the sky and chuckled. "Me? Lord, no," he said as if the idea amused him. "I'm as human as they come, and I hate the water.

Throw me in, and I'll sink like a stone. Can't even swim." He glanced at our surprised expressions. "I know, strange place to work and live if you hate the water, right? Hell, if it wasn't for my wife and kids, I'd probably never take a bath." He rubbed his hand on his chin and tilted his head to the side as he gently set the pails down. "You must be good witches if Eisheth talked to you the way she did."

"We try," I told him.

"If you're not an undine, why are you out here on the beach?" Ami asked him.

"Eisheth and I are taking care of the sharks," Joe told us, glancing toward the ocean. "She promised to take care of them the rest of the way." He shoved his hands in the pockets of his jacket and shrugged. "I don't mind taking a walk on the beach every couple of days to help these little ones." He reached into the pail and gently rubbed the small shark Eisheth had handed him. "They're so small and helpless, I can't help but do what I can."

"Sharks helpless?" Jason asked. "I wouldn't call a shark helpless."

Joe eyed Jason and then looked back out at the waves. "Most don't, but you'd be surprised. I don't know what it is, but something's killing them. Or they're all disappearing. I don't know. I don't understand it. Undine sharks and regular sharks alike." His eyes teared up. "Amelia was looking into it, but we may never know now."

"Just great whites?"

"No, ma'am. Any shark. All the sharks."

I watched him curiously as he picked up the pails again. "Are you bringing them to Charles?" I pressed.

"Charles?" he muttered, shaking his head and setting them on the sand once more. He looked down at the buckets. "No, ma'am. I'm bringing these straight to my wife, Lana. She'll take care of them herself, get them fixed up and healthy so we can get them back in the ocean. Her and my son, Remington."

I wondered why he wouldn't bring them to Charles, but I didn't ask.

We stood there motionless; the only sound on the stretch of the beach was the wind and waves. I wanted to ask him more questions, but it was not the right moment. I wasn't sure if I could trust Eisheth yet, and by extension, I wasn't sure about Joe.

I was also concerned that if I asked more (or the wrong) questions, the friendly man's mouth would snap shut like a clam.

Joe smiled. "Well, thank y'all, and good luck helping Eisheth." He nodded to the rest of us. "Nice meeting you. If you need anything, you just come by our condo. We're on the fourth floor, the wife and me. Any friends of Eisheth are friends of ours."

"Thanks, Joe," Jason told him.

As if on cue, something rushed past us, and I watched as a feathered shadow landed in the sand next to the pails, plunging its face in the water as Joe cursed. He ripped the owl from the bucket and flung Archie toward the waves before the divine predator could grab one of the baby sharks for dinner.

Joe cursed again, hugging the pails tighter as the owl flapped its wings, rising up into the air, and flew off into the night.

CHAPTER FOURTEEN

"*I* was trying to get one to talk to it, not eat it," Archie explained. The owl's head swiveled, and it looked around as if on alert. "I wasn't going to eat it. But, of course, I wasn't going to *eat* it." Archie shifted his weight from one foot to the other and then stretched his wings out and back. "What do you take me for?"

"Why don't I believe you?" Emma said to the owl.

"You can hear me, so you believe in me. It's not such a short hop, skip, and jump to believing anything I tell you." Archie's chest swelled as he puffed out his feathers in a show of intimidation. "Just take anything I say as a divine message from the goddess herself, and we'll all get along much easier."

We were standing in the parking lot between Joe's car and the stacks of wood lining the lot's edge. It was late and quiet—a few cars passed on the road, but they all drove by without stopping. Emma looked at me, and I could see she was waiting to hear any insight I had.

"I don't know," I said in response to her unasked question. "As soon as we go in there, the walls will hear everything we say, everything we talk about. After Eisheth's thing about not being able to turn against someone she's charged to protect, even if they're doing something destructive?" I glanced up at the six-floor condo building. "Fish prevented her from saving Amelia. Not *a* fish. Lots of fish. She was practically pushed away from Amelia by a school of them all working against her."

"Those have to be undines, right?" Jason asked. "Regular fish wouldn't act like that. But why would undines work against the mermaid that's supposed to be protecting them?" He frowned as he tried to make sense of the situation. "That doesn't make sense."

I nodded. "There's something you need to understand about the paranormal world," I told him while leaning against the stack. I cast a glance at Emma. "Both of you. Oaths matter in our world. Oaths that you swear, oaths that you take, oaths that are intertwined with what you are by your very nature. We don't take those oaths lightly."

"Are you saying we humans do?" Emma asked, a little offended.

"Astra is not saying that," Ami said, a half-smile on her face. "Emma, you may violate an oath, and while this is a betrayal, your only penalty may be your guilt. We are magical beings who can access, but are also governed by, unseen paranormal energies. Intentions can be hardened by these energies, which can also act as glue. So yes, we can do more than you, but we face greater consequences."

"And you humans don't take oaths very seriously," Archie added smugly. "Just look at your divorce rate."

"Considering the gods' long history of infidelity, maybe you want to back up your tail feathers just a bit, bird," Emma told Archie. "Everyone struggles. Even you. Even gods. That's just the nature of existence for everybody."

"Okay, Professor Know-It-All," Archie answered, his eyes rolling.

"Just ignore him," I told Emma. "Look, Eisheth has to protect the paranormal world in the ocean. It's her purpose, her nature. And because it's important to their survival, she protects the health of the oceans as well," I explained. "So, from where I sit, the undines would have prevented her from saving Amelia for only two reasons. One, they believed that by killing Amelia, they—the undines—would be safer. Or two, the undines—or some of them—have joined forces with someone else to oppose Eisheth."

Emma tilted her head. "So even if she knows why, she—"

"Can't tell us. Not even to save herself."

"She would betray what she is sworn to protect," Ami added.

The three exchanged glances.

"I don't understand what sharks or an underwater casino have to do with any of this," Ami said, her eyebrows furrowing. I noticed she was clutching her tarot cards tightly. "Or Amelia's relationship with Eisheth." My sister looked at me. "That card comes up over and over again. Eisheth and Amelia's love for one another is somehow the center of this. I can feel it."

"After what you just said, you don't see it? I can see it clear as a bell." Emma looked back and forth at us both, her expression slightly surprised. "Wow, sometimes you can't see the magical forest for the sparkly trees, can you?"

I frowned. "Quit being insulting and just spit it out, Emma."

"Your cousin hexed people to have bad luck, turn into chickens as punishment for misdeeds, whatever, right?" I hesitated for a moment but then nodded. "Now, okay, granted, she did it for a valid reason, presumably—but she *hexed* people. Whoever she wanted, for whatever reason she wanted. So she's not bound by who and what she can and can't hex just because she works for the undines, right?" Emma looked back and forth between Ami and me, her expression incredulous. "Really? You don't see it?" Emma turned to Jason. "How about the other human here. You see it?"

Jason looked baffled as Ami shook her head no. He said, "We know she's a hexing witch, but I don't see—"

"Oh my gods," I whispered, my eyes wide.

"Astra's got it." Emma nodded. "Right in front of your nose, right?"

"She's a hexing witch in a relationship with a mermaid that knows there's something bad happening to the mermaid's charges in the ocean.

Something bad that Eisheth can't stop because of her obligations," I said slowly, rubbing my head with the gloved palm of my hand. "Eisheth can't tell us what's happening because the perpetrators are under her protection. But Amelia could have stopped them for her with a hex—"

"Could have. Can't anymore. A dead witch hexes no fish people," Archie said quietly.

We all fell silent for several minutes, and I walked a short step away from the others to the edge of the wood stack where moonlight splashed across the beach. I looked out and was struck by how lonely it seemed, like it was mourning Amelia's loss and waiting for what might happen next.

"How did I miss that?" I whispered.

Paranormals were so frustrating.

And I say this as a paranormal.

We are frustrating, with frustratingly large blind spots—a weird mix of modern woes and medieval constraints all wrapped up in ancestral obligation. You know, the military had a department of scholars tasked with keeping up with all the unwritten rules of the various clans and species as their internal regulations and cultures of origin changed—and boy, did they struggle.

Those nerds often looked more haggard than soldiers in the field.

"I understand why you did this," I said softly, looking out over the water. "But you can't protect everyone; you can't guarantee everyone's safety. The world isn't like that anymore." I wasn't sure if I was talking to Eisheth, Amelia's spirit, or the goddess that gave me the star power. Or maybe me. "One person can't stand against—"

I stopped myself.

"No, Astra, one person can't," Ami said, walking up to me. "But that's why we have covens." She smiled. "We just have to work together, that's all."

Her words, meant to be supportive and comforting, nearly caused my heart to stop in my chest. Then, I felt the color drain from my face as the last piece, the last *why*, clicked into place.

Ami stared at me, alarmed. "Astra, are you okay? What, what did I say?"

"Covens. Witches working together." I turned toward Ami. "Amelia was killed because of us. She had to be. Why would whoever wanted her dead wait to kill her until right before we showed up? It makes no sense. We're a complication."

"Unless they did it because you were coming," Jason, who'd joined us, said.

My thoughts raced, but my hands were still. "It does make sense. If you think you're about to go from fighting one witch to five, and two of those witches have powers that can discover who you are?" I stared at the ground, a lump in my throat.

"Oh, no. No, no," Ami's eyes teared up. "They thought we were coming to help her."

"So they killed her before you arrived," Emma said, her voice infused with a tone of finality that somehow made the revelation worse. "Who knew you were coming?"

I turned and glared at the cheerful yellow fish tank building. "Charles."

* * *

WE STORMED into the marbled lobby, dimly lit due to the late hour. The recessed aquariums held few fish, but the fish I could see were all oddly fearsome-looking.

Charles Undine sat behind the reception desk, the chandelier casting a warm glow across his features. He looked so relaxed. You'd never think someone was just murdered.

"We know you did it," I said quietly, deciding to just open with an assumptive accusation.

"Did what?" Charles asked, the smile fading, his face now creased with concern. "Astra, what are you talking about?" Charles's deep-set eyes bored into mine, never wavering. He sounded hurt, confused.

No. Ignore the puppy dog eyes.

It had to be him.

I jabbed a finger toward him from across the desk. "Oh, please. Tell me you didn't kill Amelia. You were the only one that knew we were coming. The only one she would have had to tell to get us our keys."

Charles shook his head, a flash of anger in his eyes now. "I don't know what you're talking about, Astra," he said, standing. "I would never—"

Ami reached out a hand and gently pulled me away from the desk so she could take my place. "Charles, Astra told us who you are—the caretaker of the undines in this hospital. Yes? Is that accurate?"

The handsome doorman stared at her and then nodded.

"We believe Amelia was killed because some people thought we were coming to help her. Eisheth is unhappy with some undines for some damage she perceives they will do to the ocean, and we think Amelia was going to help her ensure that whatever they were doing would not take place." As Ami spoke, the fish swimming haphazardly behind Charles gathered slowly around him, creating a sparkling halo of sea life. "We also don't think they knew exactly who was behind this, and they thought we were coming to help uncover that information. You, or someone you told, did not want that to happen."

"Back off the C-man," an angelfish snapped, swimming up to the glass in quick, jerky motions. "He's just doing his job here. He didn't do anything to Amelia."

"Then who did?" I asked the fish. "Someone did."

He fell silent.

"If that's true, that's—" Charles's voice caught in his throat. He clenched his fists. "Look. I don't know much about any of this. You have to understand I'm an undine that spends most of my time in my human form. I'm one of them, but..." He glanced back at the fish tanks, his expression wistful. "I'm not in the water enough to be..." Charles sighed and collapsed into his seat behind the desk. "Look," he said again, frustrated. "This is a punishment. My role here? It's a punishment."

He gestured toward the chairs in front of the

desk and in the waiting area alcove against the wall. One by one, we plopped down into them.

"I was offered a variety of places to serve out my sentence, and I chose this one. It is isolating, yes. And I never get to the water, but this penance position, at least, allowed me to do some good." Charles sighed. "I wish I could have done something for Amelia. Really, I do. But I didn't know anything was happening, and, as I've mentioned, I am not in control here."

"Who is?" I asked him.

"The owners."

Did he mean the residence owners of the condo? Before I could ask Charles to elaborate, Jason asked, "Why? What are you being punished for?"

"I fell in love with a human," he answered, his eyes softening. "An undine can't fall in love with a human. They can't be together here. Or there." He gestured toward the fish tank. "It doesn't work. But I couldn't help myself. I wanted to be with her so much. She was the most beautiful thing I'd ever seen, and she chose me. Do you understand how special that is? How magical?"

Jason and I glanced at each other. He half-smiled at me.

"What happened?" Emma asked as Ami blinked sympathetic tears away.

Charles shook his head. "I followed her onto shore, and I lived with her. I married her. I thought we'd gotten away with it. I stayed away from the ocean, from lakes. I thought no one would know." Charles looked down sadly. "A few years ago, a hurricane flooded our houses, and undines swam in...they told the royal family. I was given a choice. Go with them and make amends, or my love would be given Undine's curse."

My sister gasped in horror. "They would take sleep's breath from her," Ami whispered.

Ondine's curse — or, more officially, central hypoventilation syndrome — is an often fatal respiratory disorder that occurs during sleep. The syndrome got its common name from an old German story, which was popularized by the 1811 novella "Udine" (later made into a play called "Ondine"). A story that, of course, was more fact than fiction in. many ways.

Not all cases are caused by the curse of an undine—but once in a while?

They are.

Charles nodded. "Something that would torture her while she lived and kill her eventually.

And so I left her. And I serve here. I am bound to serve the undine just as Eisheth is. And so I could do nothing for Amelia, and I can tell you nothing."

"Because?" I asked sharply.

"Because they could still go curse the woman he loves, Astra, you know that," Ami said, her hand on my arm. "It's why he could not help Amelia and won't tell us who killed her now. If he even knew anything—and since he's a prisoner of a sort, I doubt they confided in him."

"Who's they?" I asked, looking directly at Charles.

"I couldn't help Amelia, anyway. I don't know who killed Amelia," Charles said. He dropped his shoulders, his face weary, suddenly. "It's true; I couldn't tell you if I knew, and it was an undine. But I promise you, I do not know who killed her. I'm glad of that, honestly. I would not want to decide between protecting my love or honoring my friend."

I looked at Charles, his slumped shoulders and tired face indicating more truth than my psychometric grasping of his hand could. "I don't understand. If you couldn't help us and you owe allegiance to the undine, why did you protect us from the police when they showed up here?"

The doorman made a disgusted sound in the back of his throat. "I don't assist selkies. Ever. I don't care how much help and support Saul has given the bosses or how much he supposedly protects this place from being scrutinized too closely." Charles's face scrunched up with distaste. "Ever since he showed up here, and they all started working on the underwater casino together, the hospital has been filled with wounded undines."

I blinked.

* * *

WE WENT UPSTAIRS to Amelia's condo after Charles left the conversation to attend to his late-night responsibilities. It was exactly as we had left it, and I felt a surprising sense of relief. I was expecting to find the place ransacked.

We spread out to go through the papers we'd left unexamined from our previous research. "Over there," I pointed toward a table.

Jason nodded.

"Are you sure you saw a bunch of fish drown Amelia?" Ami inquired as she shuffled through the casino-related papers Althea had left on the table. "Based on what Charles said, it sounds far more likely the selkies drowned her." She frowned. "I couldn't believe he just mentioned that almost off-handed at the end."

"I know, right? I almost choked on my own spit when he mentioned that casino," Emma said. "I don't know if it's witchcraft, but you guys have the darnedest luck getting people to accidentally spill pertinent information."

"You saw Amelia drown?" Jason asked, looking concerned.

"She saw through her power, Jason. She held Eisheth's hand and saw what the mermaid saw." Ami shuddered. "It's hard enough being what I am. Astra, I don't know if I ever told you this, but I don't envy your power."

"Huh. That's a weird thing to say." Emma stood up from the papers she was scanning. "Isn't it more or less the same?"

My sister shook her head. "My visions are hazy and sometimes symbolic. Astra sees things as they were seen with no symbolic metaphors, no hazy softness."

"You still both see visions. Does a filter make that much of a difference?"

"If my powers wanted me to know someone died, I might see their body lying on the ground. Astra's more likely to see them stabbed and gasping for breath." She shuddered. "I see the thing I need to see to understand what I need to know—and I have no idea what decides that. The gods, the universe?" She shrugged. "Astra clearly sees what has imprinted the most energy on what she is reading."

"Right." Emma continued shuffling papers. "Still seems similar."

Ami's expression looked slightly put out, as if she was bothered by Emma's lack of attention or her flippant dismissal of our magical differences. "Negative emotions, such as fear or terror, generate the most energy of any emotion."

"Yeah, I think I saw a Disney movie about that once." Emma tapped the table and looked thoughtful. "Interesting. Your powers sound much more polite."

Ami turned away from Emma and rolled her eyes demurely. "Anyway, Astra, you didn't answer my question. Are you sure you saw fish drown Amelia?"

"Yes," I said, looking up from where I was shuffling through Amelia's hex book. But then I came to a halt and pondered it. "Wait. No. I saw them, a swarm of them, blocking Eisheth's path to Amelia beneath the water. But I didn't see how Amelia got into the water."

"You mean a school," Archie corrected. "Bees swarm. Fish school."

"Actually, fish shoal if they're together," Ami told him. "They school if they are all swimming in the same direction."

"No one cares," the bird snapped back.

Ami narrowed her eyes. "What's got you so grumpy?"

"Do you know how hard it is to find something to eat here? Everything I see could be an undine. I'm exercising an incredible amount of self-control! I'm starving here!"

Ami moved toward the kitchen to get Archie something to eat.

"So what is it they're really building out there?" Jason said. "Is it an underwater casino?"

I nodded. "That's what the papers say."

Jason's eyes widened in surprise. "I thought you went out on the boat."

"We did."

"Didn't you go check what they were building?"

Ami and I looked at each other as she fed Archie strips of beef jerky. "No, we just went out on the water to ensure we weren't overheard by the undine." I pointed to the wall. "They're right on the other side, so they can probably hear every word we say." I tapped my fingers on the counter. "We didn't think to, honestly."

"Maybe we should." Ami held up Amelia's datebook. "Coordinates are the final entry before she died. I put them into my phone, and it appears to be about three miles off the coast. I think Amelia went out to visit the construction site."

"Is there a name? A notation as to what they mean?"

Ami shook her head. "Just three Xs. Like she didn't want to write it down."

"So is that three people, or one person?" Emma asked.

We all looked at each other.

"Who wants to take a boat ride?" Emma asked cheerfully.

CHAPTER FIFTEEN

*A*part of me wished we could have brought Mitzi to the location. After all, she was a shark, and the four of us were not only an incomplete team, but we were also air-breathing creatures attempting to unravel a mystery that might lie beneath the surface of the ocean.

But Mitzi's mother had been adamant about getting her away from here.

I had to assume getting her away from here might have something to do with the underwater casino being built in national waters (despite the fact that an underwater casino shouldn't really be built in national waters).

So I left her back at the Vegas-style hotel with Althea and Ayla.

"Thank you," I said as Jason assisted me into the boat.

He gave me a brief grin, but I could tell he was trying to psyche himself up for the confrontation that might await us out in the darkness. Anxiety bubbled beneath the teacher's shield of calm, and his hands shook an infinitesimal amount with anticipation.

"It's going to be okay," I told him, reaching for his hand.

"I'm good. Really. I'm fine. It's just—"

"What are you doing?" a shrill voice asked.

I looked down toward the dock to find the silver-haired Parking Lot Karen staring up at me, her face an exaggerated mess of nosiness and judgment. She had her hands crossed in front of her chest, and her mouth was twisted into a smug smirk.

"Taking the boat out for—"

"Don't you think it's a little late to go on a cruise?"

Before I could answer, Joe Tiburon walked a little way out on the dock and called out, "Lana, leave those kids alone. They've got a right to go out on the boat if that's what they want. The ocean's open twenty-four hours, you know."

"But, Joe—"

"Hey, Joe!" Jason called out cheerfully.

Karen twisted her face into a mask of fury, turned on her heel, and stormed up the dock, saying to Joe in a voice loud enough to be heard by the whole cove, "You know what? I can't even talk to you right now. I can't believe you'd let them go out there. You know what it's like out there. It's dangerous."

"That's Joe's wife?" Emma asked as she came to stand beside me. "That nice guy we met in the parking lot?"

"I guess so," I said.

"What is her problem?"

I shrugged. "I have no idea. I think she's just one of those people that can't keep her nose out of other people's business without somehow putting herself in charge of it all."

"Oh, come on. I'm sure they're very nice people," Ami said. "She's just a little bit judgmental. And he did say that his wife takes care of the sharks that need to be healed. So she can't be all bad."

I could see Parking Lot Karen—oops, Lana—standing on the dock beside Joe, her face turned away from him so he couldn't see the anger in her eyes. He shook his head and touched her arm, but she jerked away.

"That isn't nice," Emma said.

"No," I agreed. "But their marital issues are not our problem. Come on." I turned toward the waves. "We have somewhere to be."

The four of us settled into the boat and cast off. Emma grabbed the throttle, and we motored out into the blackness of the ocean.

* * *

THE LIGHTS FROM THE CASINO—STILL under construction—lit up the ocean with a strange, hazy glow. It was a little creepy, to tell the truth, but my nerves were already wound like a clock spring, and I couldn't let the strangeness of it all bother me.

It was, after all, what we'd come out here expecting to find.

The waves gently rocked the boat as we motored around the outside of the half-built platform. Because the moon was bright, the building's metal walls both blended into the shadows and shone with an almost eerie glow. The interior lights, which were turned on, made it easy to see through the windows.

"It's a lot smaller than I thought it would be," Emma said.

The sizable octagonal structure appeared to float on the water, but I could hear metal against metal clanking as if chains were banging against a large hollow pipe. Though larger than the boat, it was not big enough to be a casino, not by a long shot. Instead, it appeared more like a decent-sized research facility or a small military structure. It was also oddly shaped. If you looked at it in a certain way, it resembled a push-pin or a thread spool, with the top and bottom being slightly wider than the center.

Finally, when I looked through the windows, I could see nothing resembling a casino. There were no tables and chairs, no slot machines, no chandeliers, no stages, or anything else. It was a plain and straightforward interior, all white—and it looked finished.

"I don't get it," Emma said, straining forward and squinting. "This is supposed to be a casino that will make millions? How? I doubt you could fit a hundred people in there. I mean, it's big, but it's not that big."

"I agree," Ami said. "It's not very big at all. Something seems odd. And surely there should be someone here. Where are the workers? Where is the security?"

"Security?" I asked. "You mean, like private security?"

"There should be some here, wouldn't you think?"

"Here's what I don't get," Jason said. "Why would a casino be so hard to get to? Why would they want it all the way out here? Sure, an underwater casino is cool, but three miles from shore? What's so special about three miles from shore?"

"We thought it was where state jurisdiction ends," I told him.

"Yeah, it could be that, but maritime law and jurisdictions for crimes are weird, complicated things depending on the crime and the victim and where they lived and the ship's port," Emma said as she turned around. "It's not as straightforward as plunking something down in a part of the ocean and murdering someone hoping you'll get away with it." She looked around. "Besides, this is still the United States. Federal law still goes, and that's arguably riskier than state law. But in any case, just figuring out who has jurisdiction over a crime requires the consideration of many different factors."

"We weren't thinking of crimes at the time," I told her.

"But maybe we should have. Maybe that's why it's here. To muddy the waters, so to speak," Ami offered.

"I'd assume they intend to commit a crime just from what you told me," Emma pointed out. "That's no casino. And we still don't know for sure what this thing is."

The metal door to the structure swung open with a loud screech, revealing a man in a black suit holding a gun. "And yet you came out here anyway, bumbling into things that are none of your business," a voice said.

"Who's there?" I asked.

The man stepped over the lip of the entryway and out onto the narrow platform surrounding the strange floating octagon in the middle of the ocean, the moonlight washing away the shadows that hid his face. "I thought for sure you'd run back to Forkbridge after I told the town you were with your cousin when she died."

"But we weren't with my cousin when she died," I told Detective Saul Marcus. I moved forward, my eyes on Marcus's drawn gun, to stand in front of Jason, Ami, and Emma. My bulletproof uniform was only as good as my ability to position myself in front of my family. "We hadn't arrived in town yet." I gestured toward the structure. "What are you doing out here? I don't see another boat."

Saul laughed, but it sounded more like a bark. "I wasn't planning on being out here long enough to need a boat." His eyes rolled to the structure behind him. "I just wanted to check this out. See if I could find out what the hell it was. Things don't usually stay hidden from me for long."

I blinked. "Wait a minute. Charles said you were working on the casino with the owners. If that's true, how do you not know what this is?"

"Does this thing look like a casino to you?" he asked, waving his gun toward the decidedly un-casino-like structure. "I was supposed to be keeping regulators away, and in return, I'd get a piece of the action." Detective Marcus looked annoyed and sounded angry. "I haven't seen one dime from this stupid place, and then the owners picked up and disappeared from the condo this week. No notice. No note. Not even a text. I got stiffed and duped. Or duped, then stiffed."

"I still don't understand why you would cast suspicion on us," Ami said. "You had to know we didn't have anything to do with Amelia's death."

He glared at her, lowering his gun. "Thought maybe you were being sent out here to take out anyone who knew about this place." He looked back at the structure. "That would include me. Hoped to run you off before anyone else died. Including me."

"Maybe you should have found out what this was before you agreed to be a part of it."

"Maybe you should have left well enough alone," Marcus said. He looked from me to Ami to Emma. "You could have vacationed at Disney World. I hear Hawaii is nice this time of year. You could have just gone home and let the police handle the situation here."

"It was a murder," I said. "How could we let that go?"

"Pardon me," Jason said, stepping forward slightly. "I don't mean to interrupt, but I have to ask—Detective Marcus, there's no boat out here. Nothing you say seems believable. Clearly, you got here somehow." He looked around. "How did you get out here?"

The detective raised his eyebrow at me. "Human?"

"Yes, he's human," I responded. "You're not, I take it?"

I was impressed with how careful everyone was not to mention that Charles told us Detective Marcus was a selkie. Of course, Emma and I had been trained in interrogation techniques, so we both knew not to bring up any unconfirmed information first. But Ami and Jason were just participating based on instinct, and neither had piped up to repeat what Charles had said.

"No, I'm not. Well, not entirely. My mother was a selkie, and my father was a human." He shrugged. "A detective like me." The detective looked down at the water thoughtfully. "Things were a lot simpler in their time, you know. The Witches' Council would have had this handled before anyone got hurt." Marcus coughed. "Well, except for the people they wanted to be hurt, jailed, or killed." He looked back up at us. "In any case, though, it was just supposed to be a simple job. Keep people away from this place, and the undines would pay me handsomely."

"But then they disappeared," I said.

Saul Marcus looked over the water and nodded his head. "My mother once told me that I was safe when I was on land, but when I was in the water, I needed to keep my wits about me. Those other paranormals took advantage of selkies, not to mention that we were food for some of the ocean's most powerful predators." He shrugged. "I guess she was wrong. A predator doesn't have to be big to get you, and they can still get you on land."

The detective holstered his gun.

* * *

I THOUGHT Detective Marcus would be the villain in this story, but the more he talked, the less my beliefs held water. Despite his behavior (and the gun he had pointed at us), his selkie nature wasn't really known for criminal mastermind capabilities.

Selkies (like seals) were, on the whole, just like people—some bold, some shy, some playful, some serious. But natural aggression and true fighting are rare between seals. (Well, except between competing males during the mating season.) They can share space with other species, but they generally don't interact with them, only showing aggression if threatened.

Seals and selkies mostly wanted to be left alone. They wanted food, and they didn't want to be someone else's food. Detective Marcus's prominent jowls and girth (coupled with the lack of a wedding ring) indicated he had no unique issues in those departments.

I looked across the waves.

I was expecting Eisheth to appear once we were on the water, but the mermaid was nowhere

254 | LEANNE LEEDS

to be found. In fact, the water around the metal cylinder was unusually calm. There were no fish splashing. I could only hear the wind, the waves, and the clanking of the metal chains.

We descended the ladder one at a time and stepped onto the platform.

"Who do you think killed Amelia?" I asked the detective.

"She was killed?" Detective Marcus asked. "I thought she just died."

"No, she didn't just die. She was murdered." I frowned at him. "Weren't you the one that said she died under mysterious circumstances?"

"Well, yeah, but I just said that to make you go away." He looked at me with a guilty face, then added, "So you wouldn't come out here and check out the place. Which, you know, is what I was supposed to do." Detective Marcus frowned. "If they're not going to pay me, though, they can just suck a sea turtle egg. Undines are always trying to take advantage of selkies." He pointed toward a door. "You going in?"

I hesitated.

As sincere as the selkie sounded, this could be a trap.

"Astra, can you read the structure with your magic vision thing?" Emma asked.

I shook my head. "It's in water," I told her. "Water represents cleansing, literally. Salt, too. Saltwater?" I pointed toward the waves. "That thing has been wiping away energy imprints off the outside of this thing every ten seconds. I wouldn't get anything off the outside. Or the inside, either, possibly." I looked toward the door. "Maybe there will be something in there that's not affixed to the structure I can try."

"So you can't read things that are burned. Or things in the ocean," Emma ticked off, carefully moving toward the entrance on the slippery platform of metal. "I swear, if air cleansed, you wouldn't have any power at all."

"Air does cleanse, Emma," Ami told her absentmindedly. "Just not in the same way."

"And she still has the lightning fingers," Jason told Emma almost defensively.

"Right, for all she bothers to use it," Emma responded.

"She's fine," Archie snapped. "How often do you shoot people?"

"It's not—"

"Can it, Sullivan." The owl's feathers ruffled, and Archie gave a hoot of indignation from his perch on the boat's railing. "You don't know whether it's the same or not the same, do you? Nope, you don't. So just zip your lip."

Archie settled on my shoulder just as I entered the central column of the structure. His talons gave my shoulder a small, supportive squeeze. "I hope something isn't nailed down," he murmured. "This is super creepy."

The interior consisted of a small circular room that stretched the entire width and length of the structure above the waterline. It was white-painted and covered in a thin layer of dust. One part of the floor had a light blue throw rug, and a shiplap divider divided the room in half.

It reminded me of the interior of an old battleship—had the battleship been redecorated by someone preferring a coastal boho design scheme.

"This is it?" Emma asked. "A white circle room?"

"This is all I could find," Detective Marcus nodded. "I dove into the water, and there's a pretty thick column going down to the ocean floor to anchor this thing to this spot. But that's it."

"What's down the trap door?" Archie asked, his big eyes glued to the rug.

Marcus jerked his head toward the owl. "What trap door?"

"The one right under there," Archie said, still staring at the covered floor. Then, finally, he flew from my shoulder, landed on the floor, and pulled the rug a few feet to the right. "It's right there. Can't you see it?"

Our attention was drawn to the polished surface of the painted metal floor. After a few moments, one by one, we all looked up and stared at each other, hoping that someone else had seen what Archie seemed so determined was there.

"Archie, are you all right?" Emma asked.

The bird thrust its wing toward the spot on the floor. "It's literally right there staring you in the face. Just open it. What are you, blind?" Archie flew over to Detective Marcus and hovered in front of his face. "You're a man. It's just a simple mechanical feat, but you can do it."

The detective looked dubiously at the bird. "You're an insulting yap little thing, aren't you?"

The owl flapped its wings in an agitated manner. "I'm a truth-teller. It's right there," Archie exclaimed.

Emma looked at me, then at the floor. "You know, he is an owl. They have excellent eyesight. Maybe he can see a shadow or outline or something that we can't?" She walked over, dropped to her knees, and her hand hovered over the spot for a moment. "Hey, owl, some help here? Some direction, maybe?"

"Push," Archie said, flying back down to stand next to her. "Right about here, I think."

Puzzled, Emma nodded and pressed her finger against the floor.

A large square of the floor popped up.

Emma looked up at me and smiled. "Got it." She leaned forward and peered down. "It's dark, but I can see—"

Then the floor gave way beneath us, and we were on our way down whether or not we liked it.

CHAPTER SIXTEEN

$\mathcal{W}$e tumbled through a narrow metal chute that descended a long way, a jumble of wings, arms, and legs. I only vaguely knew how far we fell, but I was very aware that my face was buried in someone's armpit when I landed with a series of thumps and groans.

I pushed off Jason, who'd broken my fall with his armpit, sat up on my elbows, and looked around.

The room was a vast cavern illuminated by oddly eerie electric lights. A concrete floor and rock walls appeared natural, with dozens of metal brackets holding lights to the walls like bioluminescent wall sconces. The ceiling was painted, but unusually—almost as if it was attempting to mimic water. Large tubes ran through the roof and along the walls emitting a soft blue light that glistened off everything it touched.

"What is this place?" I asked. I took off my glove, reached out, and touched the cement floor, hoping to get a tiny flicker of an image. It took a few seconds because I realized the most astonishing thing about the place.

I had no magic.

None.

Even if psychometry fails to do what I want it to, I'd usually get flickers and flashes of something. But here?

Nothing.

"You can't read that, Decanus," a cheerful voice called from the corner of the room. "And it will be staying that way, too."

I rose to my feet and turned toward the sound of the voice.

Sitting on an old, knobby wooden desk was the man I'd seen following us through the Kennedy Space Center. The men of the Firethorn Development Corporation. "Who are you? Where are we?"

Out of the corner of my eye, I could see Emma racing around to help everyone up and ensure there were no broken bones or bashed heads. Despite the fall feeling like it went on forever and the floor's composition being solid enough to shatter bone, none of us seemed hurt.

"Who I am isn't important. Well, I am important. Very important." The man sat down on a small chair and kicked his feet up on the desk. He had a nice, athletic build that was dressed down in a black T-shirt and jeans. The man adjusted his glasses with one hand. "What"—he grinned—"or more accurately, where you are doesn't matter either. You're here, and you're not getting out."

Ami, now on her feet, gasped as she stared at the man. "You were one of the men that took Mitzi's mother. On the Firethorn Development Boat! I saw you in a vision!"

"Yes, well, you won't be having any of those down here," the man told Ami with a raised eyebrow. "As I told you. Who I am doesn't matter."

"Fine, you don't matter." Emma moved toward him, her own back ramrod straight. "What do you want from us?"

"That's not what I said." The man stared at her with a slightly offended look, then turned to me. "I don't want anything from you. I didn't come and kidnap you. I didn't bring you here. Did I?" He shook his head. "Nope. You came out here, in our ocean, and stuck your nose to where it doesn't belong. I didn't ask you to come out here. You did that all on your own." He tapped his forehead twice, his expression bemused. "You should have gone home."

Emma's eyes narrowed. "You speak a lot for someone who claims he doesn't want anything from us."

"Lord Remington, quit playing around," Detective Marcus told the smug young man. "You won't be able to keep all of these people here. They aren't sea paranormals. Those two are humans, and you're aware of the rules. You have no authority over them." He looked around. "Where are Guy and Joli?"

Remington. I knew that name.

He was one of the condo owners.

"Lord?" Emma asked, her face surprised.

"Seriously?" Archie added. "If that guy's English, I'm a bald eagle."

"Guy and Joli are serving the cause in another way now," Remington told Detective Marcus with an expression of cruel triumph. He glanced at the tubes on the wall. "It's just us now, my friend."

"Who are Guy and Joli?" Ami asked, confused.

"You mean who *were* Guy and Joli," Emma whispered. "That guy's face says a lot more than his mouth."

"What are you talking about?" the selkie asked, his expression conflicted. "Where are the other owners of the Elysium Condominiums? You know the rules, Remmy. They're the regional deacons. There have to be three. You have to include them."

"Ah, that's where you're wrong, Saul, old fellow," Lord Remington responded, ignoring the rest of us. He stood and walked toward the center of the room. "Now I make the rules." He gestured to the cavern with the odd tubes along the walls. "Here, I have all the power. Those witches? The other owners? You? None."

"What are you talking about?" I asked him.

Remington turned and faced me. "Your people chased us down for so many years we had to create places we could hide. Places your magic couldn't reach us. Did you think we would just let the Witches' Council rule over us forever?"

The Witches' Council that was dismantled two years ago?

That Witches' Council?

I could have told Lord Psycho he was a day

late and a dollar short to participate in the inter-species coup and was working hard to protect himself from something two years gone, but I didn't. Instead, I watched and said nothing.

"You can't do this." Marcus shoved his way to the front. "Ocean paranormals are creatures of the sea. You can only keep them here if they're willing and help you out, but you can't force these people to stay here. They're humans. They're witches."

Remington shrugged. "Fake news. I can do what I want."

Emma stepped in front of Marcus and pointed toward Remington. "Let me try and parse through all this. You're an undine?"

"I am the leader of the undines in the Atlantic and Pacific Oceans," Remington said. "Well, one of them. A prince, if you will. Newly come to power thanks to my mother's choice to retire." He threw an arm wide to indicate the vast chamber. "This is one of our sanctuaries."

Emma nodded and haphazardly brushed the dirt from her jeans as if Remington's answers weren't compelling enough to get her full attention. "Right. Cool. Cool. So, why do you need sanctuaries, if you don't mind my asking?"

"I do mind you asking, actually, but I'll tell you

just the same because I'm a nice guy." Remington turned to face me. "You, on the other hand, should stay out of my business." He turned back to face Emma. "Her Council wants to get rid of us. They want us to suffer for what we did in the past."

"It wasn't my Council," I said in a noncommittal tone.

"And what did you do in the past?" Emma asked.

Out of the corner of my eye, I noticed movement in the tubes as Remington rambled on. The blue in the tubes was so light and almost blinding that I took a minute to realize the activity I was seeing wasn't light. It was fish.

No, not fish.

Sharks.

Hundreds of them.

I stared, transfixed, at the sleek bodies of the creatures swimming in the blue glow of the glass tubes. It was like a highway of sea creatures all moving in the same direction, one after another. With a cold hunger that was almost palpable, their dark, flat eyes looked out into the cavern when they could.

"Emma..." I whispered, touching her shoulder.

She turned around.

I pointed. "Look."

"We need sanctuaries," Remington said finally, "because we are trying to live in peace. We do not ask for trouble."

"Is that what the sharks are doing in the tubes?" I asked. "Living in peace?"

"Sharks don't want to live in peace. Sharks want to eat anything that moves," Remington said fiercely. He looked around the room slowly, his eyes shining in the dim light. "Fortunately, they can serve the undines by maintaining this sanctuary." The prince looked with disgust toward the tubes. "Whether they want to or not."

* * *

REMINGTON HAD no problem explaining the sharks' tubular purpose to us because he had no intention of letting us go. From his ramblings, I gathered that as sharks are the most electrically sensitive animals on the planet, the ones in the cave tubes formed a kind of sensitive barrier that ensured anyone psychically linked to the undines (like Remington) would know well before anyone approached.

"It also helps the undine royals—me, obviously —remove sharks from the open ocean. Both undine and regular sharks," he added. "I have only been in power a few months, and already I am on my way to bringing peace and freedom to the entire world beneath the waters!" His expression was self-congratulatory, and he pointed again to the tubes like they were some kind of despotic trophy case.

"Wait a minute. Why would you want to remove sharks?" Jason asked, frowning. "Sharks are considered a 'keystone' species. This means that if they are removed from the food chain, the whole structure could collapse."

Remington shrugged. "I doubt that. That sounds like fake news to me."

"No, he's right. Without sharks regulating the ecosystem underwater, vital habitats would undergo serious damage," Detective Marcus said, frowning. "And what is all this, anyway? You and the owners told me this would be a casino!" he continued. However, his voice lacked his previously displayed conviction.

Remington smiled widely. "Yes, we say a lot of things."

"What was the point of the casino cover story?" I asked him. "Why go through all the regulatory paperwork and approval and whatever to build this—"

He laughed. "We didn't do any of that," he said, waving my words away.

"But we read a newspaper article about it," Ami told him. "You had to if—"

"We found a stupid reporter, provided fake documents, and they wrote an article about it. That article got picked up by other outlets, reported repeatedly, and no one bothered to check whether any of it was real."

Jason frowned. "I don't understand."

Turning, the prince walked the perimeter of the room. "We didn't have to actually do what we said. We just needed evidence this was a casino 'being built' so no one would ask questions. We could show the articles to anyone that showed up." He frowned. "Though that didn't work with you people," he added, his voice heavy with sarcasm.

"Which people?" Ami asked.

"Yes. Witch people."

"What are you talking about?" Detective Marcus asked. "You said you were building a casino...I mean, we had plans, a site plan, and blueprints and everything."

An enormous smile spread across

Remington's face. "Yes, it was convincing, wasn't it? Like I said, what's easier? Coming up with a plan that promises everyone what they want, or actually doing it?"

Detective Marcus's face fell. "The whole thing was a lie?"

"Wow, he's a first-rate detective," Emma murmured.

"The casino ploy motivated you to help us, didn't it? I mean, you even lied to your partner for us." He pulled out his phone and tapped on it, then held it up. "Fake stories are so believable. It's so easy to lie, isn't it?" He frowned, dropping his phone. "That's why witches are so frustrating. Their stupid magic powers can sometimes cut right through a carefully constructed reality."

I watched Remington walk on, his hands clasped behind him, his gaze darting this way and that. The undine were supposed to be a quiet and introverted species, but he didn't seem to mind having a captive audience or pontificating so much I was worried the cavern would run out of breathable air.

"Your plan seems ridiculous, Remington. Not only that, your motivations sound completely fascistic. This whole thing seems to have been concocted to capture and kill sharks. You've gone to war against one particular segment of a population *you* were entrusted to care for. It's your job to lead, to protect—"

"It's my job to rule," he said in a voice as dead as his eyes.

"Okay, Tuna Hitler," Emma snapped, her face angry. "Astra's right. You can't subjugate an entire portion of the ocean's population. One, it's wrong, and two, it has consequences to the ecosystem."

"You're starting to bore me." Remington stopped at the center of the floor and gestured to the tubes. "The sharks are part of my plan. They're doing their part for the undines, in their own way. In a way we royals decide. They're useful for keeping out people we don't want to have here. Why not use them? It's better than simply killing them out of hand, isn't it? Obviously, I'm protecting them." He pointed. "Don't they look safe?"

Remington raised a hand to point but slammed his other hand down on a button. A clear glass tube shot up from the floor to the ceiling without warning, trapping us. Jason, Ami, and I rushed forward, slamming into the glass walls, but it was too thick to break.

"Let us out!" Ami shouted.

"You're wasting your time," Remington said. He strolled over and looked through the glass to us. "It's staying there. Those tube walls are completely impenetrable. No one can get in. No one can get out."

Suddenly, cold water foamed in through tiny holes in the floor and rose rapidly.

"Oh, that's not good," Emma murmured, her eyes wide.

Remington bowed to me with fluid grace. "Don't worry, it will be over soon. Your cousin Amelia saw this worked and worked well."

I banged my hand against the glass wall angrily right in front of Prince McSmug's face, but he just smiled at me. He didn't even flinch.

I could hear Jason's whisper despite the blood pounding in my ears. "We're going to die in here." He didn't sound panicked. He sounded resigned.

I looked at him. "Stop it. Don't give up. Think."

"Well, not me. I'm not dying in this place," Detective Marcus said, and in the blink of an eye, he turned into a seal. Then he barked.

"No, not at first, but even seals can't hold their breath forever," I muttered, my words lost in the sound of the rushing water.

I looked up to see if there was any space at the

top of the tube we could climb out of, but there wasn't.

"Everybody stand back," Emma said, her expression narrowing slightly. "And duck."

She pulled out her gun and fired high at the glass. The sharp sound of the bullets cut through the sound of running water, but the glass wall remained intact. She aimed once more at the tube in the same spot and watched helplessly as the bullets ricocheted off the thick glass surface in a shower of sparks.

"Okay, I'm out of ideas," she admitted, her voice a bit less confident.

"There's only one way out of here," Remington said. "And it's not that."

The water was now at our waists, on a slow march toward our chests.

"Water," Archie mumbled, his eyes wide as he stared down. "I hate water."

Ami gasped as a wave of icy liquid engulfed her, soaking her clothes and weighing her down. She was much closer to the problem than the rest of us because she was shorter. "I'm fine," she gasped again. "For now."

"We're all fine for now." Jason sank down, the icy water creeping up his torso, threatening to crush his resolve. "But if we don't figure something out soon, we need to take stock of who here can swim and who can't."

Archie stood on Jason's head, glaring at me. "You planning on trying something, or are we just going to wait for them to find our bodies?"

I inventoried the small magic items in my belt, pulled out an air bubble, and whispered the word that would deploy it. Once my fingers released the pebble, it plunked into the water and dropped through the water to the ground. Still a pebble.

"Magic doesn't work here," Remington told me with glee.

"That guy is really getting on my nerves." I looked up at the owl. "You have any suggestions? I'm all ears."

"The gods aren't magic, you absolute *dolt* of a witch!" Archie screeched as the seal formerly known as Detective Marcus splashed him accidentally. "Goddess power isn't magic! Do you really think the gods laid waste to cities and turned people to stone because they had a better repertoire of spells? Seriously? They're gods, you absolute ninny! Use the stupid divine power!"

I took a deep breath and tried to concentrate on the power of the goddesses Athena and Astraea. I didn't have time to stop and question anything—

Huh. I guess people are right.

There are no atheists in foxholes.

Or water-filled tube holes.

I summoned my faith (which, with only two feet to go before the water swamped me, wasn't a struggle), my connection to their power, and channeled it through the palms of my hands—not knowing what I was supposed to do with it.

I did think two words and only two words.

Help us.

I felt a tingle, and when I looked down, white light was glowing from my palm. Instinctively, I raised my hand and pushed it toward the glass. Much to my relief, the glass where I'd touched it cracked and melted, creating a small hole.

As water rushed out of the hole, I saw horror spread across Remington's face.

"Yeah, that's right, you royal buffoon!" Archie shouted with glee. He then let out a screech so loud I thought my ears would bleed. "Think you're going to drown Athena's very own owl? I don't *think* so!"

"It's working, Astra. Keep going," Ami whispered over my shoulder.

Feeling very strange, I kept my hand pressed to the glass and watched as the small hole grew larger and larger, the glass of the tube, once clear and bright, now frosted as if it were made of broken shards of ice.

Part of me was surprised it was happening—I wasn't doing it, not really. Something else, maybe even Astraea's power itself, was responsible for saving our lives.

Even so, I felt drunk with the energy I wielded.

"Yes! Yes, bring it!" Archie shouted. "You're going down, you over-rated, pompous, royal clod!"

"Archie!" I said, glancing at him.

"Sorry," he mumbled.

As the glass broke down even more rapidly, I thought that maybe Archie was right. Perhaps I didn't need to control my powers as much as I thought. Maybe I didn't have to be cautious with it.

I just needed to believe in it. I just needed to believe in the goddesses.

I believe in you, I heard Astraea's voice say.

It was the first time I'd ever heard the goddess's voice in my head.

Unless I imagined it.

I continued contemplating whether the voice was real, but the glass shattered with a crack before I concluded one way or another. The water gurgled as it rushed out.

"You stupid morons!" Remington shouted from outside the glass. "What did you do!? You broke it! You broke everything!"

"Astra?" Ami said, coming to my side and wrapping her arm around my shoulders.

"I'm fine," I said, but when she looked at me, it seemed she could tell I was far from it. I felt shaky and weak like I'd been pushed to the edge of something great and yet terrifying. "I'm fine," I repeated, taking a deep, cleansing breath.

"She's fine," Archie told Ami.

"That was pretty impressive, Arden," Emma told me. She looked down at the gun on her hip. "And you? You and I are going to have a talk later." She gave the gun a little slap with her hand. "I'm very disappointed in you."

"We're not out of the woods yet," Jason said, pointing toward Remington. The prince of the undines sat on the floor nursing cuts from flying glass shards. "He can't be the only one involved in this."

"He's not," I told Jason.

And then my eyes widened.

"Yes, I am," he told me sullenly. "I killed or betrayed anyone else involved. And I'm not sorry, either," Remington scoffed. "That's what always used to drive me crazy about you witches, you know? You're so arrogant, so sure that you know everything and everyone's beneath you. It's so infuriating, and I think—"

"Handcuff him," I told Emma. "Put him on the boat, and the rest of you move back from this thing a few hundred feet." I glanced at the cavern walls. "I'm going to free these sharks, and then we will take Lord Remington to see his mom."

"His mother?" Jason asked, looking confused. "Who's his mom?"

CHAPTER SEVENTEEN

"What floor are the Tiburons on?"

Charles looked up to find me frog-marching Remington into Elysium with an iron grip while Archie perched menacingly on my shoulder. Ami, Emma, and Jason followed me, each with confusion painted clearly on their faces.

"The fourth floor?" he answered as if asking another question. His tone held a tentative mix of nervousness and uncertainty as the doorman took in the scene and tried to parse what, precisely, was going on. "Can I help you with something?"

"I'm your king now, you stupid idiot!" Remington snapped at Charles, his tanned face mottled with rage. "Obviously, you can help me get away from this witch! Lock down the Elysium! Capture the witches! If I can't get out of here, none of us will make it out alive. They'll drown us all in these tanks!" His eyes, wide with panic, darted to the fish in the tank. "Someone help me!"

No one helped him.

"You're not the king of anything," I said, turning him toward the elevator. "If you don't want to be turned into a toad, you'll let Charles go back to work so we can visit your mother."

Charles looked back and forth between Remington and me as if weighing his options. "She'll be happy to see you, I'm sure." He paused. "Well, maybe not in this state. Could someone be so kind as to explain to me what's going on?"

"No!" he said, pulling on my arm and trying to flee. "I don't owe you any explanation—I am your king! Help me! I order you!"

No one helped him.

"Who is his mother?" Jason asked again.

Charles's eyes narrowed in a confused yet cautious gaze. "Lana Tiburon," he told Jason. "He's a member of the undine royal house. As is she. Now my questions, if you don't mind—what are you doing with him?" Charles turned his attention back to Remington, who was trying to squirm free of my grasp. "Has he done something to offend the Witches' Council?"

Seriously? Charles, too?

"For Athena's sake," I said as I tightened my grip on Remington's arm. "Don't you people get a single paranormal newspaper? Get visitors from beyond the mist? Keep up with things?" Charles looked slightly offended but didn't answer. "There is no Witches' Council anymore. None. It's gone. One of the circuses took them on, things went off the rails, and now the paranormal world is being run by a bear shifter and a bunch of his buddies."

"Well," Ami said, holding up her finger. "It's not quite that—"

"Oh, great, we go from witches wanting us dead to being ruled by salmon-eaters," one fish cried out from behind Charles. The fish began schooling as if the lot simultaneously decided to pace from one end of the tank to the other. "We're always the last to be considered for anything! Just because we live under the water—"

"Astra, I swear," Ami mumbled, glaring at me. "There is no need to panic! The Council running the paranormal world is now multi-species. The bear shifters are not the only ones in charge.

Everyone is working together with vampires, witches, elves, shifters," Ami explained to the fish. "Those that serve and rule do so because the paranormals of their clan entrusted them to do so."

"Hold on, hold on, back up a minute." Charles's face morphed from confusion to shock. "Are you telling me the paranormal world is now a democracy?"

"I'm saying that the paranormal world is now a multi-faction system of leadership where anyone can play a part in the government. Any species. Not just witches," Ami responded. "And we choose them. So...yes, I suppose I am."

"But that's crazy! It's unworkable!" Remington shook his head, his words coming out in a long, low rumble. "Not only that, it threatens my future. I want to be the king of something!"

"Let's go talk to your mother about that," I told him coldly.

A look of horror crossed Remington's face. "No." He stopped struggling, and his eyes went wide with panic. "No, you can't do that. You can't tell her anything. You don't understand what she's like. She will take back my title if you tell her there's no Witches' Council!"

"Boy, he went from king to frog prince real

quick, didn't he?" one of the fish asked as it swam by.

"I'm sure he's exaggerating." Jason was trying to be the voice of reason. "Why would the Witches' Council have anything to do with the undines?"

"Someday, you should let Astra tell you about her former bosses," Emma said with a snort. "There wasn't much in the world the Council didn't think was its business."

"There's no need to come up, dear," Lana called from the end of the hallway as she descended a narrow staircase next to the elevator door. Ayla, Althea, and Mitzi walked down behind her. Bringing up the back was Joe Tiburon, a pained look on his face. "I already know what shameful things you've done with the title I passed down to you."

* * *

AND SHE'D FOUND out from my mother.

Sort of.

From what I could gather? My mother, Aunt Gwennie and Aunt Gertie suddenly felt we were in grave danger. Aunt Gertie, being a ghost, was charged with finding Ayla as fast as her spirit could fly, to get the skinny on what was happening. "I figured it was you, not us. I knew exactly where you guys had gone, so she went out to look and report back," Ayla explained.

I nodded. It made sense. "But how did you know to find Lana?"

"So, the funny thing about drowning," Ayla said, glaring at Remington. "It's traumatic. People need some time to process—especially when they're betrayed by someone they trust. Aunt Gertie met the other two Elysium deacons out there on the water. They told her some of what happened, saw you guys do your Houdini impression in a big glass tube while the mad king ranted and raved, and once she was sure you were all okay, she brought them back to Jason's hotel with her."

"They filled us in," Althea added. "As soon as we put it all together, we came over here to talk to her. Once we all exchanged information, the picture of what was going on was pretty clear."

"Yes, thank you, Ms. Arden, for freeing the sharks that my son had enslaved." The cold woman I'd dubbed *Parking Lot Karen* blinked back tears as she looked at me gratefully. She wrapped her arm around Mitzi and squeezed the girl's arm. "All of the undines are of equal value to all the others, from the smallest herring to the largest whale." Her face fell. "It appears I failed to teach my son that."

"Mother," Remington whined in a most un-king-like way. "I didn't—" Lana glared at him as he tried to stand taller and straighten his spine. "I just wanted to return to the old ways! I was just protecting the small fish from the predators, and the people, too and—"

Lana wasn't having any of it. "You hurt the very people you were entrusted to protect," she said with more than a hint of anger.

"I just—"

"You engaged in cruelty. You subjected our people for your own selfish gain, for your ego. You shamed me. You shamed our family. You shamed the undines."

The rest of us stood in stunned silence as we watched the drama come to a head before us. Remington's head was bloated with arrogance, while Lana's was held high with dignity, her eyes blazing in defiance. The son may have said he was king to anyone who would listen, but Lana spoke like a true queen.

"Oh, get over yourself," Remington told his mother. "It's not your time anymore. You're not queen anymore. Like it or not, there's nothing you can do about it. And if there's no Witches' Council?" he sneered. "Nothing this witch can do about it, either."

"Are you so sure about that?" Lana asked, her voice still strong and unwavering. She didn't move. Didn't even blink. "After all, if there is no Witches' Council, then I have no rules about when to pass down my role. So you were not wrong in thinking we can make our own rules once again, son."

Remington froze.

He knew this.

He'd said as much.

But he clearly hoped his mother had forgotten.

"You betrayed the undines." Lana said the words in the same level tone as before. "You meant to hurt. You meant to harm."

"But Mother—"

"No," Lana shook her head. "You are no royal son of mine. Therefore, I disown you for the purposes of the royal line of succession of the royal house of the undine."

"You can't do that."

"Can't I?"

"Huh. I guess there really is always a bigger fish," Archie murmured.

Remington's expression turned to panic. "You can't do that!"

She made an odd movement with her hand and spoke words of a spell in a language I didn't recognize. Then, with a steely glint in her eyes, Lana brought her hand down in a sharp, vertical slash. Remington's head and chest glowed in tattoos of fish and oceans and symbols I'd never seen before.

"Stop it! You can't do this!" Remington's face fell as he looked around at his fellow fish. "They're not going to listen to you! You can't disown me!" he cried out. "I'm the king! It's my right!"

The symbols lifted off his skin, shimmering bright gold, and flew back to Lana.

Lana raised her hand and silenced him. "You are no longer king."

Remington's body trembled as his head shook from side to side. His lip quivered as he tried to look away from her. "I—I—you can't do this —you—I—"

"You're sorry, I'm sure." She stepped forward and placed her hand lightly across his brow. Then, blinking back tears, she whispered, "You're also your father's son, Remmy. Perhaps he can teach you what I could not."

Remington glowed briefly.

"Now," Lana said as she stepped back from him. "I think it's time you apologized to this child. You stole her mother. You frightened her. You made her face the world alone. Apologize, human."

His head snapped up.

"Oh, snap," Emma whispered.

"Remington," Lana placed her hand gently on her son's head after the silence dragged on. "You are exiled from the Blue Ocean, the home of your ancestors, the way you exiled the sharks from their ocean. You will suffer and struggle for the pain you caused until you learn humanity, until compassion touches your heart. Start here, my boy." She leaned forward and whispered, "Please."

Remington looked at the floor, refusing to speak.

Lana stepped back, her voice even more firm. "How can you make yourself worthy of my forgiveness when you refuse to even try to make amends with the ones you hurt most?"

Remington's head jerked up again as he glared at his mother, then at me. He swallowed, then moved so quickly he was a blur. "I hate you both," he raged, jerking free from my grasp and running out the door.

I moved to give chase.

"Stop, Astra Arden of Forkbridge," the queen commanded before I got a foot closer to the glass doors. "He has lost his place with our people. He can do little damage wherever he goes now."

"Little damage as a human?" Emma scoffed. "I beg to differ."

"Emma is right. Humans can do a lot of damage, and he's just lost everything, your highness," I asked, my eyebrow raised. "Do you know humans very well?"

"Aye, I do," she whispered and looked lovingly at Joe Tiburon, who had stayed in a back corner as if he'd been apart from the drama in the lobby. "My husband, human though he is, still loves me. He loves me for who I am, for all I am—"

"More than ever," Joe whispered, stepping forward and wrapping his arms around his wife.

I glanced at Charles, who looked pained in his silence.

"You see," Lana continued, "an undine, a mermaid, and a human can change the world together if they really try. That's what my husband and I did with Eiseth's help. Instead of fighting against the humans, we chose to assist them in the changes they needed to make." She shook her head. "But as queen, my first duty is to my people. And with that in mind…" Lana smiled at Mitzi.

Mitzi smiled back. "I can go see my mom now?" Mitzi asked with excitement.

"Of course," Lana smiled at the young shark. "I'll take you. Eisheth is, no doubt, waiting for us at the dock. She'll know where your mother is."

"Will you guys come out on the boat tomorrow?" Mitzi asked, her eyes full of excitement. "I want you to meet my mom!"

"Absolutely," Ayla told her.

Althea squeezed Ayla's hand, tears brimming as she watched the little girl. "We'll see you tomorrow, squirt."

Lana blinked away tears and moved toward the doorway. "Thank you for freeing the sharks, Astra. We will take care of them."

"That we will. And yes, thank you, Astra," Joe kissed me on the cheek. "You're an amazing girl." I winced at being called a *girl*. "Your goddess would be proud of what you helped us do here. You and your companion." Joe boinked Archie affectionately with his forehead.

Archie, to my surprise, didn't seem to mind.

"Thanks," I told him. "I hope so."

He turned and looked at his wife, the queen of the undines. "Are you ready?"

BRING YOUR BEACH OWL | 291

"Yes," Lana's voice sounded sad. "Take me to her. We have much to discuss."

The queen and her husband walked out of the building, little Mitzi between them. Lana looked down at the child and smiled, bending to lift Mitzi into her arms. "She is a perfect little angel," said the queen.

"I know," her husband replied.

"Your mother will be so proud of what a brave girl you were," Lana said as the door closed, leaving us in silence in the lobby.

"Wow," Althea breathed.

Ayla let out a deep breath. "I know, right? That was intense."

"I agree, but I'm still confused about one thing," Jason said, turning toward me. "How did you know Remington was Lana and Joe's son?"

* * *

AYLA EXPLAINED the biggest clue to Jason as we all rode up to Amelia's condo in the elevator. A clue that came before any of us knew anything was wrong at the Elysium Condominiums but one we both homed in on at the mention of a queen.

On the first day we arrived at this strange

place, Lana Tiburon told me to call her *your highness* with no clarification or explanation.

I thought it was because she was an egomaniacal woman with a stick so far up her butt she thought she was royalty, but it was, in fact, nothing more than her way of informing us she was one of the undine royals.

Lana believed the Witches' Council was still intact, and I, in my military uniform, would have had to know who she was.

But I didn't.

That *your highness*, though, was the key to it all.

The elevator dinged, the doors opened, and my mother and Aunt Gwennie jumped from the couch, their faces lined with relief to see us all safe and unharmed. "We were worried sick about all of you," my mother gasped, pulling back from a tight embrace to look closely look at Ayla's face. "We came through the communication cauldron. Are you all right? Gertrude's explanation for what was happening down here had me worried sick!"

"I'm okay," Ayla laughed. "I'm okay."

"Sorry, Mom," I said. "We're all okay, though."

"What happened?" my mother asked. "What happened down here?"

"It's a really long story," Ami said.

"And we're exhausted. It's been a long night. But, we're all okay, and that's what counts," I said, sitting down on the sofa. "We'll tell you everything that happened tomorrow when we have more time."

"We have time now," my mother said, looking pointedly at us.

I stared up, my eyes half-closed, and then closed them, leaning back on the soft cushions. "I can't go through all of this. Getting all those sharks out wasn't easy, even with Astraea's star stuff. Someone else tell it."

Between Ami and Ayla, they told my mother about the undines being unaware that the Witches' Council and all of its draconian rules were no more, Lana passing her rulership power to her son, and his decision to enslave all the sharks to power some undine underwater sanctuary while wiping out the shark population of the oceans he ruled.

"Well, that's just stupid," Aunt Gwennie said, frowning.

"That's not the half of it. He concocted the story of the underwater casino being built to explain the construction out there in the ocean. Or something." Ami frowned. "Honestly, that part just seemed ridiculous, really. But it was nothing more than a red herring."

"It was made of herring?" Aunt Gwennie asked, confused.

"No, I mean—"

"Don't be silly, Gwen. The sharks would have eaten the herring. So what happened to the sharks?" my mother asked.

"They're free," Jason said. "Astra released them all from the tubes."

My mother pursed her lips and shook her head. "Well, I'm glad it all worked out. I still don't understand why Amelia didn't tell her undine employers that the Witches' Council was gone. "

"She might not have known," I pointed out. "She was a rogue Hex Master for hire. Those folks weren't exactly looked on with favor. I think I arrested a few."

My mother frowned at the reminder of my previous life. Then she tilted her head. "Where's the selkie detective?"

"He didn't want to come with us back on the boat," Ami shrugged. "Said he would swim back. He wanted to go meet with the other selkies about Remington's betrayal. King Crazypants did lie to him and then try to kill him, so it was understandable."

"What's going to happen to Remington?" Aunt Gwennie asked.

"He's human now," I said, shrugging. "I imagine he's going to have to work through that. He went from king of a paranormal people to a run of the mill human—"

"Hey!" Emma said, looking offended. "Being human does have some disadvantages, I'll admit, but I'm not run of the mill."

"My point exactly," I said. "Remington's going to have to deal with all of the stuff so-called normal humans have to work through. The self-esteem issues and insecurities, the identity crises."

"And you don't have those?"

I chuckled. "Not the way you people do." I lifted my hand. "I'm just saying, that's a big change. I'm sure he's going to have to work through it."

Emma looked at me with an expression that contained affection and deep doubt. "Sure. We'll just pretend that's true, Ms. Astra Vainglorious."

Ayla chirped out a laugh. Then, glancing at me quickly, she silenced it.

Aunt Gwennie stood. "Well, it's late, and I'm sure you all need some sleep. Your mother and I are going to head home. Minerva and I will contact all of you tomorrow through the regular phone unless something comes up."

"Yes, that's a good idea," Jason said. "I really need to take a shower and get some sleep."

"I understand you have a hotel room?" my mother asked, her expression stern and forbidding (in case Jason was possibly contemplating staying here with her four daughters and Emma). "Right across the street, isn't it?"

Jason smiled. "Yes, ma'am."

"And you'll be staying there," my mother said, her tone not even hinting that what she said had one molecule of a question. (In sales, I believe they call her mode of speech an *assumptive close*. As in, she *assumes* what she said renders discussion on the matter *closed*.) "Somewhere safe and clean? Otherwise, you can come back through the cauldron with us to Forkbridge."

"Yes, ma'am," Jason said, his face perfectly still and nondescript, though I could see the corner of his mouth quivering slightly in suppressed laughter. "The hotel is just fine, and I'll be fine there in the room." She continued staring. "By myself." More staring. "Thank you, ma'am."

"Of course! Of course! You're so welcome, dear. I'm so glad you're all safe," my mother said, her eyes twinkling as she looked at us one by one. "You call me if you need anything or get into trouble. All right?"

"All right, well, we'll talk to you all in the morning," Aunt Gwennie said as she led my mother to the back hallway toward the cauldron. "Goodbye, Emma."

"Bye," Emma said. "Travel safe!"

"Of course," Aunt Gwennie called back before they were out the door. Then, to my mother, she commented quietly, "What a silly thing to say. It's a cauldron. You just walk through it."

"Well, she doesn't know that, Gwen," Mom told my aunt.

"Someone should tell her. She hangs out with witches enough to know that, at least. My goodness."

As soon as we heard the telltale pop of the cauldron's connection closing, we burst into laughter. "They really can be funny when you're not terrified they're about to turn you into a frog or something," Althea said, her laughter fading. "Oh, man, why am I so tired?"

"You, too? I'm exhausted," Ami yawned, plopping down on the couch.

"Me, too," Ayla smiled. "I think I'm going to go to bed."

I turned to Jason. "You want to stay for a little while?"

Jason's gaze was drawn immediately to the hallway where my mother had vanished just moments before. "No. I think I need to take a shower and get some sleep." He leaned forward. "I'll see you tomorrow for breakfast?"

"Seriously?" I frowned, unhappy—and thought about launching into a diatribe against my mother and a reminder to Jason that we were both in our thirties and could do whatever we wanted without getting permission from anyone —but then a wave of fatigue rolled over me like a tsunami. "Okay. Yeah, sure. Probably best."

Jason smiled and stood. He leaned down, brushing my cheek with his fingers. "Good night, gorgeous. You were pretty badass tonight."

"I'm pretty badass every night. You, too, by the way," I said, smiling up at him. "I'm not really the type of girl that needs to be rescued by a knight in shining armor, but it's absolutely adorable watching you try."

He chuckled.

Jason walked over to the elevator, smiled at Ayla and Ami, and then turned around. After a brief moment of preoccupation with him, I sighed and turned around to face the rest of the group.

They were all looking at me, their eyes wide.

I wrinkled my forehead at them. "What?"

Before any of them could answer, Archie gave a rumbling snore from his perch on the dining room chair, and we all burst out laughing.

CHAPTER EIGHTEEN

"$\mathcal{D}$o you think she saw the news this morning?" Althea asked me.

"Who?"

She cocked her chin toward Lana Tiburon, who was standing on the bow. Lana seemed curiously content for a mother whose son had just been arrested for murder, as the sea spread out before her like a sheet of glass. "If she did, she doesn't look too torn up about her son spending the rest of his life in a Florida prison."

Looking at her, I saw a flicker of anger in her eyes. "I don't think it's that. I think she's resigned because Remington has consequences to face for what he did," I said. "But I'm sure she still loves him. Besides, it seems Detective Marcus compromised on his revenge. Remington was only charged with manslaughter in Amelia's death."

"And they'll probably plea bargain it down to negligent homicide," Emma added, placing her hand on her chin and looking away. "Prosecutors have no spine."

Detective Marcus hadn't returned after leaving us in the sham casino, but I'm sure the gossip about what happened between Lana and Remington had spread like wildfire shortly after it happened. Everyone had to know what happened by now, between the newly unleashed sharks and all the underwater witnesses to Eisheth and Lana's meeting last night.

Marcus, I presume, learned about Remington's freshly gained human status and wanted to assist him in becoming acquainted with the facets of human punishment.

According to the reports, Marcus arrested him before the sun came up.

"There's one thing I don't get," Ayla said, plopping down on the bench next to me. "Why was Lana so upset about you parking in the parking spot Amelia told us to park in? Like, I don't get it. What's so important about a parking space?"

"That's my fault," Lana's husband, Joe, called from the bow, interrupting what appeared to be a lengthy and emotional conversation between him and Jason. "I hurt my back changing a light bulb a few weeks earlier. Parking in that space meant the fish stuff was a bit closer to the dock, and I didn't have to carry it as far." He smiled. "No big conspiracy."

My sister nodded. "That explains that. But why did Amelia want us to park there?"

As the boat sailed through the water, I reflected on it. Leaning back, I closed my eyes and imagined the parking lot from every perspective. "That spot is the only spot that blocks the view to the path down the beach," I said, opening my eyes. "If she was coming back from the beach and didn't want to be seen, a vehicle there would accomplish that."

"She could also jump into the Jeep and get out of Dodge if she needed to," Althea said. "With that stack of wood by the fencing, none of the security cameras would have even picked her up." Thea looked at me. "I think she knew someone was after her. She wasn't sure she could trust us, but it seems like she hoped she could."

"She should have known she could," Ami said quietly. "We were family."

I leaned back against the bench and thought about it. "I wish she'd trusted us, too. If she'd just told me what was happening when I talked to her about our visit, we could have gotten down here sooner, and maybe she'd still be alive."

"When you talked to her in your military uniform, you mean," Ami said, pointing to my Decanus outfit. "Just because you took off the patch doesn't make it not a military uniform, Astra. You're walking around in an outfit that most people associate with the Witches' Council —and fear. You just assume everyone knows what happened in Imperatorial City. Maybe she didn't, either." Suddenly, Ami half-smiled sadly. "Believe it or not, some of us try to ignore the paranormal world from a political standpoint."

"Yeah. You know, the way you ignored the coven for thirteen years?" Ayla added.

"And Mom?" Althea chimed in.

"And us?" Ami said, bringing up the rear of the speeding accusation train that came at me from all sides. "All sisterly recriminations aside, Astra, there's something about it that makes you seem like you're from a different world," she added, looking pointedly at my outfit. "You keep the Council alive just by wearing that."

"That's a lot to put on an outfit," I told her,

shifting uncomfortably on the seat. "I don't mean anything by it. It's comfortable, it's defensive, and it's got a lot of sentimental value, but I don't see how it makes me a symbol of fear."

"That's because you were part of the regime and not subjugated by it," Ayla told me as she crossed her arms, her teenage face a perfect picture of arrogant judgment. "You're not that scary, Astra, but to a lot of people, that outfit is."

I'm not that scary, huh?

I wondered what Ayla would think if she knew I really was capable of being absolutely terrifying when I wanted to be.

Though maybe they had a point—most of the time, I didn't want to be anymore. I'd been a soldier for a long time, and I suppose in my line of work, it's necessary to lay on the intimidation, even when you don't want to.

Yeah. Maybe they had a point.

This clothing has undoubtedly generated a lot of confusion over the last two days. Plus it could have been the reason Amelia was hesitant about confiding in us. That reason alone was enough to give me something to chew on.

"I'll think about it, okay? That's all I can promise."

* * *

I STEPPED AWAY from my sisters and headed toward the stern to think about what they'd said. I stood there for a few minutes, watching the white wake behind the boat and thinking. Suddenly, I felt familiar talons pinching at my shoulder. Archie's wings opened up and folded against his sides as he bent down to talk.

"I hate boats," Archie grumbled. "Too much weird wind. The ocean, too. Water. Unless I have to drink it. I mean, I have to drink it." He leaned forward and twisted his head at an angle impossible for anyone other than an owl. "Can we vacation inland next time?"

"You got it," I told him. "Hey, I wanted to ask you something. You said the gods weren't magic. Like, their magic wasn't magic. What did you mean?"

Archie thought my question was the funniest thing in the world. His chest shook like a bowl of Jell-O as he turned his shoulders toward me and attempted to straighten up after his laughing fit. "You really missed witch Sunday school when you were a kid, didn't you?"

"I was not into the religion, no," I told him, glaring. "Morality is doing right no matter what you are told. Religion is doing what you're told no matter what is right. That, by the way, is an H.L. Mencken quote—and no," I said, heading the brag off before he could claim ownership of it, "he didn't get it from you."

"Moral certainty is always a sign of cultural inferiority. The more uncivilized the man, the surer he is that he knows precisely what is right and what is wrong," Archie said in response. "Mencken said that, too. And he did get it from—"

"No, he didn't," I said.

"Okay, yeah, no. He didn't." Archie watched me patiently with his big, round eyes. "First, I'd like to point out the military is all about doing what you're told—so your issue isn't with obedience, it's with who you're willing to listen to."

I didn't respond, but for the second time today, I had to admit that someone else wasn't wrong in their observation. "God magic, Archie?"

He cast a knowing glance at me and nodded. "Magic is what witches do, yeah? They manipulate the energy that binds the world together to force things to happen or see things in that energy that others can't. But there are limits. Agreed?"

I nodded.

"The energy isn't good or bad. It just is—like clay to be molded or paint waiting for a brush. What happens isn't about the paint or the clay. It's about who holds the brush, who molds the block. That can be learned. It can be used for whatever the witch decides, even if it's bad. That's arcane magic."

I nodded. "But that's not what the star energy is?"

He shook his feathered head no. "Divine magic is sourced from a god. It is *granted*. No one has access to it inherently, and no one can *learn* it just because they want to. It's a gift, and it's not really magic in the sense that magic is energy. Understand? It is colored by the gifter."

"And the gifter is Athena—"

"No." He cut me off with a sharp shaking of his head. "The gifter is Astraea. It is her essence you hold, her power you wield. Athena's just standing in because Astraea booked out when the humans broke her heart. That—her leaving—was a permanent decision. But even when gods die or leave, their power doesn't abandon this place—it transmutes into something else. You have that something else. Well, you and other folks. But the others don't dilute what you can do."

"So that's why I was able to do something even though Remington had somehow blocked magic in the cavern."

Archie nodded. "That's right. You were able to summon 'magic' because you have divinity at your fingertips. You're literally a walking, talking conduit for divinity."

I looked out over the water. "I never asked for this."

"You keep saying that. Or thinking it. And I keep telling you—no, but you agreed to it."

"But why me? I'm the least of all witches from any gods' perspective." I pushed the hair out of my face and scratched Archie on the head before dropping my arm. "I don't like using it. I don't know what to do with it. I don't know what it can do, so it's hard for me to count on it. It's like being given a weapon with no manual."

"It's for you to figure out."

"Fabulous," I muttered.

"It's you and Astraea. Together. As a new force in the world. I mean, if you are a conduit for divinity, and divinity is, well, it's divinity, it means you have access to energies, to knowledge, to the wisdom of the universe and the other universes, too. It's something you have to figure out. You have the tools." He shook his head again.

310 | LEANNE LEEDS

"Look, I don't know how else to explain it to you." He shifted on my shoulder. "I don't have a star living in my gut."

I chuckled, and Archie's serious expression changed. He nuzzled me. "You know, it might be easier to have an inner goddess if you dressed better," he told me as he ruffled his feathers. "I mean, no offense, your sisters are right. That uniform is horrible, and you look like a soldier of fortune in it."

You would think if I really did have a goddess in my gut, a superpower, and had just saved three square miles of sharks, people would be less inclined to criticize and more inclined to compliment.

But apparently not.

I said nothing, though. I just replied, "No offense taken."

Archie shrugged. "I'm just saying that if you want to inspire people instead of making them feel they've been cornered by a fierce and terrifying authoritarian soldier sent to dominate the little people, you might want to put on a dress once in a while." He glanced down. "And take off the actual jackboots."

* * *

"THAT'S ASTRA! The one in the scary uniform!" Mitzi called from the water.

I winced.

The little shark bobbed alongside a much larger, fiercer-looking beast I assumed was Mitzi's mother. The larger great white had to be at least ten feet long. It swam around in the water, tailing and corkscrewing to get a better view of the boat. Her scars glistened silver in the sun as if she radiated an inner light.

"Hello," the larger shark said. "Thank you for helping my daughter."

As I nodded, Eisheth broke through the water and gazed up at all of us. "You're not so useless as I thought you would be," the mermaid said with an imperial nod. She looked directly at me. "I admit that I underestimated you, Astra. I am in your debt. For what has happened, and for what is about to come to pass."

"Thanks," I said. "I think."

"What's about to come to pass?" Ayla asked.

Eisheth raised her palm toward me, and I felt a warm glow in my stomach. Like mild heartburn.

It wasn't uncomfortable, but it wasn't subtle, either.

With her other hand, the mermaid reached

out and passed her hand over a little fish jumping alongside her. The slender fish gracefully rotated in a circle as it morphed into a beautiful young lady. Her silky hair glimmered like raven feathers over a delicate face that gleamed like the sun. I thought I saw a fin as she sank beneath the sea.

Eisheth dove beneath the waves after her.

"What the heck are we looking at?" Jason choked out.

"Astra, did you do that?" Ami gasped.

"Shhhh," Joe told him quietly. "Just watch."

We stared, mouths agape.

Eisheth ascended effortlessly from the water a split second later, her muscular tail fin propelling her to unprecedented heights. She became luminous suddenly, and as the other dark-haired mermaid rose to hover at her side, they shared a strange white light. That dark-haired mermaid looked almost like…almost like…

"It can't be," Althea choked.

"Amelia," Ayla whispered. "That's Amelia! The second mermaid!"

"That's impossible," I said, staring in shock.

"Boy, you don't listen when I talk, do you?" Archie grumbled and then slapped me on the gut with his wing. "Eisheth needed your help to do it, but it's not impossible."

"He's right. It's not impossible, I'm telling you. I can see her spirit," Ayla told me, her voice definitive as to the truth she perceived through her ability to see the dead. "That's Amelia. I'm sure of it."

For a few moments longer, the two shone. The couple then lifted their hands in a polite salute, rolled, and dove beneath the sea.

They were gone.

"What just happened?" I asked, stunned.

"Undines can jump from body to body beneath the water," Lana explained, smiling as she dabbed the tears from her eyes. "We can also aid wounded undines in this way if they choose to accept the help. The fish that surrounded Amelia, the ones you saw in your vision?"

"They weren't *drowning* Amelia," I whispered. "They were helping to move her into a safer body that could breathe underwater."

Lana nodded. "My son may have wanted to corrupt our people, but he did not."

Joe smiled. "They are still good at heart."

* * *

WE SPENT the afternoon being greeted—and thanked—by a wide range of aquatic denizens, from dolphins to sharks. And there were so many sharks—blacktop sharks, spinner sharks, sandbar sharks, black nose sharks, sharp nose sharks, bonnethead sharks, and a few more I couldn't name. It was a welcome departure from the day's routine criticism directed toward my clothes.

It also made me wonder how on earth Remington could have accomplished his master plan.

"It's too bad Charles couldn't come out with us," I commented near the conclusion of the day as we guided the boat around some pelicans to dock. "I like him a lot." I turned to face Lana. "I know he's in some kind of undine jail or work release program, but we'd probably be in jail if it hadn't been for his assistance."

"Charles is gone for a few days," Lana told me, her eyes sparkling with delight. "He's gone to get his wife and bring her back here to Elysium."

I blinked. Then I frowned. "Why now? Why put him through all that only to relent now? It almost seems cruel to do it only to shrug it off later. What if she met someone else?"

"Astra!" Ami gasped.

"What? It's true."

"The rule about the humans was from the Witches' Council. It was not one of the undines' rules," Joe explained. "The Council worried that undines mixing with humans would cause too much attention, and so they forbid it." Joe glanced at Lana. "The penalty could be gruesome if it got reported."

None of us asked.

I could imagine just fine.

"That didn't appear to concern the two of you," I remarked, a little more accusingly than I probably meant to. Though I had to admit, I'd been grumpy about the situation ever since I discovered the Queen Mother had a human husband while Charles toiled away downstairs taking care of the fish.

"I'm a royal," Lana said without further explanation.

Yep.

And to be honest, she didn't need to explain.

The powerful had their own code of norms, while those without power were held strictly to another set of regulations that the powerful would never observe. It was the same in the human, witch, and undine realms. Rulers, dictators, and kings frequently broke principles and customs that no one on the bottom rung of the ladder would even consider breaking.

Though I couldn't say I was thrilled about it, I understood.

"Charles will be happy when he gets back," Lana said with a smile. "He's been so worried about his wife and about her future. Since he's been so loyal, such a good caretaker, we've made him a deacon at Elysium, and I am happy to say he accepted." She looked at all of us as the boat bumped against the dock. "Will you stay to meet her?"

* * *

WE DIDN'T STICK AROUND to see her, though I did leave a note for Charles (and my phone number, along with a gift subscription to *Paranormal Times*).

Staying in Cocoa Beach for a vacation was no longer appealing after what had occurred. Even though Amelia was now a mermaid, her death affected us all, and the two deacons Remington had sacked (via execution) wouldn't leave Ayla alone—at least until Ayla requested a potion from Althea to keep them quiet long enough for her to get out of town.

Emma walked into the living room and set her bag down next to ours. "Well, that's it. I'm ready.

Though, if there's no room for me in the Jeep, I'd be happy to hitch a ride through the cauldron," the detective said innocently, her face a mask of indifference. "I mean, I wouldn't mind."

I tossed her my keys. "You're driving the Jeep. I'm going with Jason."

"Oh," Emma said, pretending not to look disappointed. Then she smiled. "That's fine. I think I can handle the Jeep. You have the V8 HEMI engine, right?"

I raised my eyebrow. "No. That just came out on the 2022 models," I said, trying not to look amused. "It's a V6 turbo diesel, though."

"Eh, good enough," she shrugged. "You're going to trade that in for the HEMI as soon as you can, though, right?" Emma tilted her head. "Or no, wait—I bet they have conversion kits. Yep, I'm sure of it, now that I think about it." She looked at me. "We both still have vacation days. Want to convert it to—"

"We'll talk about it back in Forkbridge," I said, cutting her off before she realized the Jeep's tires could be bigger with a higher lift.

We dragged our luggage downstairs, and I watched as the Jeep tore out of the parking lot, spraying gravel and leaving a cloud of dust behind it. Archie flew from my shoulder and landed on the hood of Jason's car, then flapped his wings.

"They'll be fine," Jason said, watching me.

"She knows I'll turn her into a frog if she wrecks my Jeep," I told him, throwing my duffel bag in the back seat of Jason's ridiculously practical sedan. The car was so short it made me feel like I was in a go-kart when we went on the highway. "Or my sisters." I sighed, carefully helping Archie settle in the back seat. "I think I need a vacation from my vacation. What a crazy few days."

I closed the back door and turned to gaze at the bright yellow siding. The dancing of sunlight across Elysium's smooth edges made me smile, and I stood for a moment listening to the crashing of the ocean waves just down the path. What strange places paranormals had carved out in the human world.

I knew I would miss it.

And that I was probably never going to eat seafood again.

"Ready?" Jason asked me.

I turned and smiled at him. "Yep."

Jason got into the driver's seat, and I climbed into the passenger side.

He cranked the engine and it sputtered to life with a loud whine.

Time to go home.

* * *

THANK YOU FOR READING!

I hope you enjoyed Bring Your Beach Owl. Please think about leaving a review! Astra, Archie and the whole Arden family continue their adventures in Book 8, Against Owl Odds.

KEEP UP WITH LEANNE LEEDS

Thanks so much for reading! I hope you liked it! Want to keep up with me?

Visit leanneleeds.com to:

Find all my books...

Sign up for my newsletter...

Like me on Facebook...

Follow me on Twitter...

Follow me on Instagram...

Thanks again for reading!

Leanne Leeds

FIND A TYPO? LET US KNOW!

Typos happen. It's sad, but true.

Though we go over the manuscript multiple times, have editors, have beta readers, and advance readers it's inevitable that determined typos and mistakes sometimes find their way into a published book.

Did you find one? If you did, think about reporting it on leanneleeds.com so we can get it corrected.

ARTIFICIAL INTELLIGENCE STATEMENT

Portions of this book were created with the assistance of AI tools used for editing, proofreading, and refining the text. However, the ideas, storyline, characters, and overall creative vision remain my own original work.

While some aspects of the cover image were generated using AI tools, it was done so under my creative direction and curation.

I want to acknowledge the use of these technologies as part of my creative process, while affirming that the essence of this work comes from my own imagination and effort.

Leanne Leeds

www.ingramcontent.com/pod-product-compliance
Lightning Source LLC
Chambersburg PA
CBHW021447240626

47153CB00001B/340